Easily Twisted

3 Curiously Dark Tales to Keep You on Your Toes

JORJA GASKELL

ISBN: 9798702061757

Cover design by: premiumsolns

Library of Congress Control Number:
2018675309

Printed in the United KingdomCopyright ©
2021 Author Name Jorja Gaskell

For Torin, who most certainly would have read this while perched atop a red phone box. May he forever enjoy his star gazing…

CONTENTS

VILLAGE FETE

Dora Proctor sat contently in her front garden, trowel in hand, as she gazed at a patch of newly sprouted daffodils. The dainty flash of yellow smiles were perfect among her already colourful garden. Dora gave a dreamy, satisfied grin then clapped her hands free of the mud that clung to her bare palms. She didn't believe in the use of gardening gloves. She found them to be far too formal. Too restrictive. They removed a person's basic need to be covered in the soft soothing moisture of the earth. Mud was a must in Dora's life.

"You alright, *pet?*" came a sudden voice from over the garden wall. Dora looked up and jumped to her feet. She smiled when she saw her elderly neighbour, Mable, hurrying across the wide dirt road that separated their homes.
"Morning Mable!" Dora waved, "You coming in for a cuppa?"
"Oh, no thanks, flower. I've got to rush off soon!" Mable leant heavily against the red brick wall between them, "I was just wondering how things were coming along for this year's fete,"
Dora shrugged.
"*Uhh*, yeah getting there, I think. I'm just waiting to get the last bits and pieces in order. How are *you* getting on?"

1

Mable gave a small grimace.

"Well actually I'm struggling to get the craft table set up," she admitted, wearily, "If you're not too busy later, would you mind giving me a hand?"

Dora gave a bright smile, "Sure thing! I'll be over this afternoon!"

Mable was about to give an enthusiastic reply but was cut off when a large black car came bouncing awkwardly over the bumpy dirt road behind her. Dora and Mable shot each other a glance.

The car made a sharp left turn and crunched into next door's gravelly driveway. The car's engine cut to silence and Dora leant over her garden wall to get a better look.

Mable raised an eyebrow as she muttered an interested, "Ooh I say!"

The pair watched on as the door of the black car flew open, and out swung a long leg. An even longer body followed.

Soon, standing broodily in the driveway was a tall, silver-eyed man in a knee-length black trench coat.

Dora stifled a gasp.

"Eeeh well," Mable flushed red and gave a girlish giggle, "What do you make of that then?"

Dora tilted her head to one side like a magpie glaring at some shiny plaything. She watched as her new neighbour slunk around to the back of his car, popped open the boot, and dug out several large leather suitcases. Luggage in arm, the man impressively managed to click shut the boot with his forehead, then awkwardly lurched up to the front door of the cottage.

Just as he reached the door, the stranger spun around and fired a scorching accusatory glare in the direction of Dora and Mable. Embarrassed, Dora averted her gaze. Mable rolled her eyes, unimpressed.

The two women watched on as the stranger, still struggling with his many suitcases, laboriously dipped to the ground, and fumbled beneath a dusty old door mat, from where he unearthed a small silver housekey. He unlocked the front door and let himself inside. With a fearsome crash, he slammed shut the door behind him.

Mable pouted, confused, and jerked a thumb towards the house.

"What do you reckon that was all about?" she asked, curtly.

Dora bit her lower lip as she thought.

"Dunno yet," she admitted, "Guess I better go find out,"

****

Sherman pushed his way into what would be his home for the next week. He had told the property owner over the phone that he would require a much longer stay. A blatant lie on his part.

Sherman kicked shut the front door to silence the vicious glow of sunlight that stung his eyes. The darkness enveloped him, and Sherman breathed a sigh of relief. Carefully, he placed his many cases down onto the ground and leant back against the door behind him. He took a cleansing moment to bask in the darkness and felt as its coolness filled his lungs. This house would be perfectly suitable. So far so good. Just as the web advertisement had promised.

Idyllic countryside holiday cottage - the perfect peaceful getaway for aspiring writers and artists.

Yes, yes it certainly seemed the part. Even in the shadows, Sherman could make out the cottage's open plan living room and kitchen. A small corridor branched out at the far side of the bungalow and led to what he presumed were bathrooms and bedrooms. He would look into that later. For now, he would rest.

In the dark. Alone.

Sherman lay down on a large plush sofa and covered his face with a pillow. And that is how he would have remained for a good while, though it was not to be. He had just gotten comfortable when there came a sudden and infernal knocking at the door.

Sherman sat bolt upright and flung away his pillow in shock.

"*Hello?*" yelled a voice from outside, "Have you got a minute?"

Sherman stared with wide horrified eyes at the door. He remained silent and hoped that the insufferable knocking would subside. He tried his best to ignore it, but the ruthless hammering didn't let up.

"Oh, for God's sake," Sherman muttered, loudly to himself. With a sneer, he relented and marched over to the door to open it.

The sunlight flooded the hallway and Sherman immediately threw a hand to his eyes in defence against the relentless golden needles. Peaking between his fingers, Sherman found that a young woman was waiting for him upon the doorstep. The woman smiled brightly in greeting.

"Well, hiya!" she exclaimed, enthusiastically, "You must be Sherman!"

Sherman smirked in confusion.

The young woman was a delicate looking thing. Small and young; at a glance she could have been mistaken for a teenager. At a very generous estimate, Sherman guessed that the young lady could only have been around twenty-one. Her hair had been dyed bright purple and was pushed back into a high messy bun.

Sherman immediately recognised her. She was one of the two females that had watched him as he arrived. Gossiping about a new face in the village, Sherman suspected.

"Shall I pop in and show you around the place?" the young woman asked, brashly, "I mean, obviously you've seen pictures of all the rooms online but the cold tap in the kitchen has to be jiggled a certain way…"

"And why exactly are you so familiar with this building?" Sherman interrupted. The young woman paused, taken aback.

"Uhh… well, I'm Dora. The property owner. We were speaking on the phone, remember?"
Sherman snorted.
"Aren't you a little young for this kind of thing?"
Dora smiled and looped her thumbs through the straps of her dungarees.
"Well, I don't think you're ever too young to have a business plan!"
Sherman stared down his nose at her and snarled, "Quite."

Dora peered around Sherman's colossal form as he loomed in the doorway. She waited for him to move aside and invite her in, though from Sherman's stoic unwillingness to budge, Dora soon realised that that was not an option.
"Well, if you change your mind, I'm only next door…"
"Listen, Donna-"
"*Dora* -" Dora corrected him, and Sherman pressed a forefinger and thumb to his nose.
"*Dora*," he sighed, his impatience growing, "Just remind me what it was you said about this place? Why is *this* cottage in *this* village the *perfect getaway*? As you so beautifully put it, that is!"
"Oh, well just look at the place!" Dora beamed, waving a hand towards the rolling greenery of the hillscapes that grew out of the horizon.
"It's very beautiful here! And so peaceful…"
"Ah yes!" Sherman interjected, sharply, "There's the word I was looking for. *Peaceful*!"

Dora shuffled awkwardly on the spot but forced a small smile.
"That's right," she nodded. Sherman shook his head.
"Well, it's certainly hard to feel *at peace* with the likes of you *capitalising* on my time! See that I am not disturbed again!"
With that, Sherman slammed shut the door in Dora's face, sealing her outside.

****

Sherman's fists trembled at his side. He pressed his brow against the cold wood of the door, sneering, hissing from the confrontation. His jaw clenched, Sherman pushed back from the door and sucked in a deep breath. His eyes flicked to the largest brown suitcase at his feet, and in a flash, he set to work in a flurry of billowing coattails.

With a click of the latch, Sherman popped open the suitcase, and out sprung a stack of foldable compartments. Sherman plunged his hands inside, a ghoulish grin rippling across his lips. From within the folds of brown leather, Sherman extracted a great sparkling ram's skull; a large pentagram etched onto its bony brow. Sherman crossed into the living room and hung the skull above the fireplace.

There was work to be done.

****

Dora waited a while longer on the doorstep in silence. There was really no way Sherman would be able to work that tap without her showing him the knack. Dora yielded with a small sigh, then turned and skipped out of the driveway. As she took a step forward, she felt a weight shift in her dungaree hip pocket. Before she could catch it, Dora's phone tumbled out of her pocket and landed face down on the gravel with a crunch. Dora stared at her fallen phone and winced in apprehension. With a tentative hand, she scooped the phone from the ground and turned it to inspect the damage.
"Oh, bloody hell!" she exclaimed as she glared at the deep fractures that split the glass screen. Dora frantically jammed the power button with her thumb, but it was to no avail.
"Great!" Dora sighed, frustrated.

Oblivious to Dora's anguish, Mable yelled over from her post at the garden wall.

"Not much of a talker, was he?" she quizzed as Dora stomped towards her. Dora knitted her brow.

"No, not really," she admitted, grouchily, "He wouldn't even let me in! I just wanted to show him around, that's all!"

Mable pursed her lips and her face shone with an odd smugness, though she said nothing. She simply waved a goodbye and sloped across the dirt road to her small cottage. Dora snorted a small laugh and rolled her eyes. Without another thought, she wandered back into her own garden and continued to fawn over her newly sprouted daffodils.

****

The moon replaced the sun in the sky and Dora had long since called it a day on her gardening. She had showered and pulled on a set of fluffy pink pyjamas. With her favourite cooking show playing on the TV, a fire roaring in the hearth and a steaming mug of tea pressed between her palms, Dora curled up into her armchair and heaved a contented sigh. She sat happily, though groaned at her TV when *Brenda from Sheffield's* souffle didn't rise.

"Rookie mistake, Brenda!" Dora yelled at the screen. She was so invested in the show that she was blind to the suspiciously flickering flame of the scented candle upon her coffee table. The flame continued its flickering. It trembled wildly and tripped over its own heat, then with a sudden hiss, it fizzled and died.

Dora's eyes shot over to the sudden swirling thread of smoke, and she realised that a cold breeze pricked at her cheek. Dora pursed her lips.

"*Weird*," she said. At that position in the living room, there shouldn't have been a breeze from anywhere. Unless the back door was open. Dora pouted, confused.

"*Huh*," she muttered as she rose from the comfort of her chair. Dora was sure that she had clicked the door shut behind her after coming back inside from feeding her hens. Dora padded into the kitchen; her footfalls dulled to silence by the colossal woolly socks on her feet. Sure enough, surprisingly so, the back door had been left ajar. Dora raised an eyebrow. It was a heavy door that made a distinct click-clack when the inner latch caught. Dora had been sure that she had heard that very sound when she had come in from the back garden. With a shrug, Dora pushed shut the door and tried to think no more on it. There came the *click-clack* and Dora rattled the door handle to test its integrity. The door remained shut tight.

Dora unhooked a giant metal hoop of keys from a cubbyhole behind the fridge. She rifled through the many jangling keys and quickly found the one that fit the back door. With the door locked and secured, Dora hung the keys back in their hideaway, then returned to the living room to watch the rest of her show. By the time Dora sat down in her armchair, the show was just ending. *Brenda from Sheffield's* deflated souffle had cost her the title, and she was being sent home in a haze of shame. Dora threw back her head in annoyance and she slapped a palm against her thigh.
"Oh, for god's sake!" Dora sighed, jumping to her feet, "Well, may as well call it a night I suppose!"

Dora took a moment to shut off all the downstairs lights and to test that all the doors were truly locked. She scurried upstairs then hit the light switch on the landing. The light bulb sparked into life for a mere second, only for it to blow and immediately die. Dora scrunched up her lips, irritated, as she stood there in the darkness.
"Oh, bloody hell!" she breathed as she stepped blindly into the bathroom. Dora's hand flailed around in the dark, until her fingers caught the cord for the light switch. With a tiny victorious smile, Dora found a better grasp on the cord, though she did not pull.

Suddenly, Dora's muscles seized in place. A biting cold numbness locked her in stone. She couldn't quite place why. Something just felt dreadfully off. Her breath rattled in her throat as she waited there, frozen in the dark, with tight metal bands of dread crushing her chest. As she poised in the pitch black, she felt as though hidden eyes were watching her. The primal fear of being stalked by some feral night beast was all consuming, and soon Dora was trembling with terror. If she turned on the light, would there be some monstrous phantom waiting to savage her? There was only one way to know for sure. Dora clenched her entire body and pulled the cord. Light flooded the bathroom with a harshness, an urgency.

Dora flinched and braced.
Nothing lay in wait. Nothing lurked. Dora was alone. No ghouls. No ghosts. Nothing.
Only Dora stood there in that bathroom, feeling irreversibly idiotic.

Suitably shaken but otherwise fine, Dora brushed her teeth and scrubbed her face with a warm flannel.
"Jeez," she muttered to herself as she crossed the landing to her bedroom. Dora flopped heavily onto the bed and jumped under the covers, nestling herself up like a cosy hen in a nest. Even with her shake-up, Dora's eyes slid shut as soon as her head hit the pillow. A good night's sleep was always something that came easily to Dora and tonight was no exception. Within seconds, a cloudy dreaminess filled her head in place of consciousness.
It was only the sound of a sudden squeak that ripped Dora from her slumber.

Dora's eyes shot open. She listened.
For a moment there was silence. Then she heard it again.
A squeak. A familiar one.
It was the sound of the handle on the backdoor being pulled.
Air whipped through Dora's hair as she sat bolt upright in her bed. She listened.

There came one more squeak. Then a rattle. Then a clattering – an aggressive, manic clattering laced with the distinct hoarse sounds of panicked breathing.

There was someone downstairs. And they were locked inside.

Dora's jaw clenched hard as her breath rushed to her in tight, panicked heaves. With a stealth to rival an alley cat, she slid out of bed and crept to the top of the stairs. At a whopping five-foot-nothing, and with the build of a Dickensian orphan, Dora didn't much fancy her chances against whatever mystery phantom lurked below. She couldn't even call anyone. Her phone was broken, and the landline was in the living room. Dora waited.

Rogue beams of moonlight found their way into the hallway below her, painting the sharp edges of the night with purposeful ivory brushstrokes. Dora squinted into the shadowy pit and waited.

Suddenly, pouring out of the wall like tar, one of the shadows broke ranks and ran.

Dora was sure that she screamed, though she heard no sound leave her mouth as she threw herself back in panic.

The huge, gangling shadow sliced passed the base of the stairs and once more melted into the darkness. There was no way Dora was about to give chase. Instead, she rolled over backwards and leapt to her feet, sprinting into her bedroom like a child fleeing from some imagined boogey man. Dora launched herself headlong into her bedroom and slammed shut the door. There was no lock, so she settled on dragging her heavy vanity table across the door as a barricade. Dora dropped down onto all fours and pressed her ear against the floor. Directly below her was the living room and as she listened, there came the sound of a window being pried open. Dora's evening meal was very close to resurfacing as she rolled over towards her bedroom window. She peered over the ledge and pressed her face to the glass, cupping her hands to either side of her eyes. As she stared down into the garden, she saw nothing out of the ordinary.

A bright, nearly full moon hung in the sky, enough light to expose anything that may have slunk away suspiciously. Dora waited. And waited.

Nothing presented itself from the darkness. Terrified and furious, Dora slammed her hand against the windowsill and turned around, sliding her back against the wall as she slumped down to the floor. She leaned across to her wardrobe and grabbed from within a sturdy high-heeled shoe. She clutched it to her chest, ready to use as a weapon should she need.

Outside in the garden, Dora was oblivious to the great, spindly shadow that slid out of her living room window like a snake. Without wasting time, the shadow zipped across the grass and vaulted the brick wall, ducking out of sight and dissolving into the darkness.

****

Dora woke with a jolt and groggily shielded her eyes from the glow of sunlight that burst through her window. She was sprawled upon her bedroom floor with a high-heeled shoe still clutched deftly in her hands. Dora sat up sharply and tossed the shoe back into the cupboard. With a determined grimace, she jumped to her feet and threw on some clothes. She had plenty of questions in need of answers.

The cottage door thundered beneath Dora's hammering fist. "Sherman!" she screamed as she continued her furious knocking, "Sherman, answer this door right now!"

After a few minutes, the door eventually creaked open and a familiar gaunt face poked out through the gap.

"Yes, Delilah?" Sherman sighed.

"*Dora!*" Dora corrected him, sternly, "Listen! We need to talk!"

Sherman's lips shrivelled back from his teeth. By that point, he was fully aware that his incorrigible purple-haired neighbour was named *Dora*. He just didn't want to give her any kind of validation.

"Unfortunately, we seem to already *be* talking," Sherman scoffed.

"No, I mean…" Dora became flustered, "Look, did you see anything suspicious last night? Someone was in my house!"

Sherman narrowed his eyes. He slid his whole body out through the gap in the door so that he could stand upon the step. He made very sure to keep the door from opening more than it needed to, and Dora instinctively backed away.

"I saw nothing suspicious," he said.

Dora raised an eyebrow.

"Are you sure?" she pressed, suspiciously, "Because someone was definitely in my house last night! And I know for certain that none of my neighbours would pull anything like that!"

Sherman's neck prickled with the beginnings of rage.

"Are you insinuating that 'twas I that crept around your home last night?" he snarled.

Dora shrugged heavily.

"Look, I don't … I don't really know! I just know that someone was in my house and …"

"I can assure you that I am not in the business of creeping through young women's houses like some common sneak thief!" Sherman barked, cutting her off, "Plus, what time would you have me down as committing such a debauched act?"

Dora's mind temporarily glowed with white noise as she tried to think back.

"Uhh…" Dora pondered aloud, "It was about half-eight when it happened,"

Sherman shook his head and gave a mocking *tut-tut*.

"Well, that is where your hurtful allegation falls flat. For you must understand that I was visiting your local public house at that time!"

Dora gritted her teeth, visible confusion twisting her face as she mulled over the words that she had just heard.

"You were… at the pub?"

Sherman chewed the inside of his lip and growled, "Is that so hard to believe?"

Dora gave a reluctant nod, "Well, yeah actually!"

The tall, glowering man sucked in a deep breath of air through his nose and hissed it out through clenched teeth in a jet of hot steam.

"Very well!" Sherman snarled, "Then it is fortunate that I have a plethora of alibis to choose from. It rather seemed to me that the whole village was there! The whole rowdy lot of them were determined that I should play darts with them. A drunken, bastardisation of the game, may I add?"

Dora shuffled on the spot and offered, "I'm sure they were just trying to be nice,"

Sherman sneered, "I shall have you know that in future, I will not be drawn into such childish antics when…"

He stopped short. Dora craned her neck forward as she waited with bated breath for him to continue. Sherman's eyes had drifted to the ground and his thin lips twitched.

"And where have you been?" he hissed.

"Eh?" Dora blurted then glanced down to the ground.

Sat serenely beside her feet was, of all things, a sleek black cat.

The cat's giant green eyes flicked up to meet Dora's as it gave a curt, *meow*.

"Oh!" Dora beamed, reaching down to pet the small creature, "Hello, princess! Where have you come from?"

The cat offered another *meow* in response.

"Is that so?" Dora humoured the little animal, and the cat began to purr.

Dora glanced back towards Sherman, whose brow had now been visited by a throbbing blue forehead vein. Dora pointed down to the cat.

"Is she yours?"

Sherman scoffed but nodded.

"Yes," he hissed, "She dived out of the car window just as I pulled into the village, I thought she was gone forever!"

Dora stared at the tall, shadowy man as though regarding a particularly abstract art exhibit.

"You brought your cat on holiday with you?" she murmured in confusion.

Sherman spluttered indignantly and bent down to grab the black cat.

"Come now, Penthesilea!" Sherman snapped. The cat was less than cooperative. She fizzed into a bristling ball of wiry fur and hissed like a cobra. Sherman snatched back his hand and stood bolt upright, his face ashen, mortally offended. His eyes narrowed as he watched the cat's fur smooth back into place. She then flagrantly began to slink around Dora's ankles, and purred as she went.

"Fine," was all Sherman had to say as he slammed shut the door.

Once again, Dora was left stunned and alone on the doorstep. Alone, that was, say for her new feline friend. The cat glanced up at Dora and *meowed*. Dora screwed up her lips to one side as she wondered.

"Pentha… Penthis… huh?" Dora's tongue stumbled over the animal's given name, "Well, anyway, I guess you can come home with me if you like,"

The cat gave a *meow* of approval. Dora smiled and tucked a hand against her hip.

"Well then, we're going to have to do something about that name of yours!" Dora explained as she bent down and scooped up the soft purring fuzz ball.

"I suppose we could call you Penny?" Dora said, as her feet crunched across the gravelly driveway.

Dora crossed her garden and let herself into her house, making sure to lock the door behind her. The black cat jumped out of her arms and trotted her way into the kitchen. Dora followed her newly acquired friend and found the little animal perched atop the work surface beside the sink. Dora crossed her arms and rested an index finger against her lip. "You don't look like a *Penny*... you're definitely a *Mittens*!" An approving *meow* sealed the deal.

The sunshine of the morning clouded over into a drizzly afternoon and, rather than tend to her garden, Dora decided that the best use of her time was to set about baking some cupcakes. Her newly named feline friend, Mittens, sat upon the countertop and watched over her work with intrigue. The small, sleek animal was occasionally given the post of quality control officer, whenever Dora offered her a spoonful of green frosting.

Dora had made sure to bake enough cupcakes for all her neighbours. It was one of her favourite activities to waltz down the street and distribute baked goods like some kind of benevolent pastry fairy.

Baking completed, Dora journeyed the short distance across the road and knocked on Mable's door.
"Mable?" Dora yelled as she looked up to the highest window of the cottage, "Are you in? I brought cake!"
There was a sudden commotion from inside, as though a frenzied gaggle of geese had been released. Within mere seconds, the door was flung open. There stood Mable in the doorway, brandishing a rolling pin as though it were a weapon.

Dora leapt back in shock and nearly dropped her tray of cupcakes.
"Whoa! What's got into you?" Dora exclaimed. Mable sneered and pointed her rolling pin towards the holiday cottage at the end of the street.

"That *Sherman* is up to something in there, pet!" Mable
glowered, "I keep hearing an awful moaning and a scraping as
though furniture is being dragged around!"
Dora pursed her lips.
"I've not heard anything," Dora assured Mable, "And my
house is closer. Surely I would have heard something too!"
Mable shook her head adamantly.
"My ears are keener than yours, young lady! I know what I
heard!"
"Alright, alright for god's sake Mable, I believe you!" Dora
sighed, touching her free hand to her head in exasperation,
"And what exactly do you want me to do about it?"
Mable fluffed up her body in much the same way that Dora
had seen her chickens do on many occasions.
"Go over there and see what he's up to!" Mable insisted,
"There's something weird about that man!"
Dora rolled her eyes and forced the tray of cakes toward
Mable.
"You don't have to remind me," Dora grumbled.

****

How long had it been since Sherman had started writing his
novel? Three years? Five years? More than that? And for how
long had his poetry been slipping into obscurity? These days,
every pen stroke seemed wasted and useless. Nothing
inspired him anymore. His muse had long since released his
hand from hers and left him floundering in the wake of her
sweet perfume.
As Sherman languished in the darkness of that godforsaken
holiday cottage, the familiar wingbeats of panic fluttered
inside his chest. What had he even achieved in his life? His
friends and family had long since disassociated with him and
now even his cat had abandoned him on a whim. It was
becoming more and more apparent that this venture into the
countryside was essential. This was the time to make his life
happen.
By whatever means necessary.

The stinging white smoke of the incense burned Sherman's nostrils as he kneeled inside a ring of blood-red candles. The curtains were drawn, and the lights were dimmed. The gentle flickering of the flames around him were his only light source. The night of the full moon was fast approaching. It would be upon him by the close of the week. Sherman needed to be prepared.

He closed his eyes and bowed forward, dipping two fingers into the small clay bowl on the ground before him. The bowl was filled to the brim with a viscous red liquid. Sherman pulled his stained fingers towards his forehead and drew a smooth line of red across his brow. He chanted under his breath. Just then, a loud knock at the front door caved through his concentration like a brick through a window. "Hello?" he heard a voice yell from outside.

Along with his concentration, Sherman's ritual was now completely ruined. Fluidly, furiously, Sherman sprang to his feet and kicked over the bowl on the ground before him, splattering the red liquid all across the walls, and knocking over a few of the candles in its path. Sherman stomped to the front door and wrenched it open, though only just enough for his head to poke through the gap. There upon the doorstep, a tray of sickly-looking green cupcakes clutched in her hands, was Dora.

Dora loitered nervously upon the doorstep, close to wilting beneath Sherman's fiery gaze. He seemed hardly a man as he loomed there - the whites of his eyes glowing, hot steam hissing from his nostrils. In that moment he was a great bull, squaring his chest to the challenge of a matador. He was ready to charge. A fury and a thirst for blood glowed bright in his eyes.

It was in that exact moment that Dora knew she had made a terrible life choice. Even the tray of cakes, which she had brought in hopes of softening this interaction, had deflated in fear.

"Look here… uhh … Sherman," Dora choked, subconsciously using the cake tray as a physical barrier, "I think we need to have a talk!"
The visibly throbbing, bright blue vein made yet another guest appearance in Sherman's brow.
"You thought wrong…" he hissed, his voice demonic and hoarse, "So… *so*… *so* wrong!"

Dora nearly bolted. Somehow, she managed to hold her ground, though she trembled in every limb. As she mustered the courage to speak up again, her eyes drifted to the liquid red stripe across Sherman's brow.
"Are you bleeding?" Dora gasped; her fear replaced immediately by concern. Sherman's eyes grew wide and white as he realised his blunder.
"No!" he insisted but his cry came too late.

Dora precariously tucked the tray of cakes under one arm and pushed her free hand against the door.
"There's a first aid kit in the kitchen, let me show you *where -*"
The door creaked ever so slightly under Dora's small hand. The action had completely caught Sherman off guard and panic sparked in his body like a whipcrack. Without thinking, he lunged forward, and body slammed Dora.

The shock and sheer force sent Dora tumbling backwards over her own feet. She fell to the ground and landed in a heap. The tray of cupcakes flew in a high, majestic arc over her head, then plummeted down to earth like a meteor. The tray bounced bluntly off Dora's face and rang with a metallic *twang.*

The smell of copper was instant, and a sudden throb of pain pulsed in Dora's nose like a second heartbeat. Still airborne, the cupcakes rained upon Dora and splattered hard over her body with a grotesque squelch.

All Dora could do was lay on the ground in stunned silence, as she heard the door of the cottage slam shut.

"*Well,* that went well…" Dora muttered.

****

Limping badly and partially blinded by the giant purple bruise that had now claimed half of her face, Dora moodily shoved her grocery basket down beside the cash register. Tom, the young shop owner, stood behind the counter and grimaced as he began to scan Dora's items.

"*Sheesh,* what the hell happened to you?" he asked, concerned, "Bad day?"

Dora grumbled, near incoherently, "You could say that!"

Sensing that Dora's abrasive side was about to make a full appearance, Tom pressed no further. Instead, he steered their small talk in another direction.

"How's everything going for the village fete?"

Somewhere upon Dora's swollen face, a smile muscled its way to the surface.

"Nearly sorted now," she replied, brightly, "Just a few more bits to get done! Mostly just the gardening now!"

Tom gave a contented nod. Just then, something occurred to him.

"Hey, your holiday guest was in the pub last night! Absolute *barrel* of laughs, isn't he?"

Dora's insides twisted at the very mention of her ghastly neighbour, but Tom's words had tied within them an extra knot of dread.

"Sherman … *was* in the pub last night?" Dora quizzed. Tom gave a keen nod. Dora's eyes narrowed.

"So, he wasn't lying…" she muttered to herself, quiet enough for Tom not to hear.

"How long was he there for?" Dora continued, nervously.

Tom blew a jet of air straight up into his fringe as he thought.

"Dunno…" he began, his eyes cast to the ceiling as he pondered, "Suppose he got there about seven and left about maybe… half-ten? Surprised he stayed that late to be honest. We were trying to get him to play darts and he was *not* into it!"

Dora managed a chuckle, "Yeah I heard about that! Sherman said it was a bastardisation!"

"We were just having a laugh!" Tom insisted, "Shawn wanted your neighbour to throw a dart at him so he could catch it in his teeth for a bet. But … yeah, we didn't end up doing that,"

Dora rolled her eyes.

"I can believe that much," she sighed, "*Listen*, did he leave at any point between the times you said he was in the pub? *Like*, did he nip home for anything and then come back?"

Tom stuck his jaw out to one side as he tried to remember. "Uhh, no I don't think so. He popped out for a smoke a few times but that was it, really," Tom concluded.

Dora gave a slow nod then bit her lip as she eyed the grey, sliding cabinet at Tom's back.

"You know what?" she said, firmly, "Give me a pack of the usual, please!"

Tom raised an eyebrow.

"I thought you'd *quit* the usual?"

Dora nodded shakily and replied, "Well I've had a weird day. I need something to calm my nerves."

Tom shrugged as he turned and dug out a pack of cigarettes from within the cabinet's sliding doors.

"Smoking is a path to an early grave you know?" Tom gave a playful wink and Dora snorted in laughter.

"Well, it's a good job I like dirt then isn't it?"

****

Dora plodded laboriously up to her front door as she struggled to cling to her giant bags of shopping. She had already made her way through two cigarettes by the time she'd reached her house, and a third was now hanging from her mouth. A gentle plume of grey smoke trailed in Dora's wake. She fumbled with the keys in the lock and pushed her way inside her home. Just before Dora could make it to the kitchen, some nagging thought at the back of her mind made her pause. Before she could comprehend why, she dropped her shopping in the hallway and scurried back outside onto her front lawn. Curiously, Dora leant over her wall and peered into the garden of the holiday cottage next door. There, sat on the doorstep with his head in his hands, was Sherman. He was tugging at his raven curls of hair, moaning softly to himself.

Dora grumbled and turned to head back inside. It wasn't her job to babysit Sherman, nor was it to even bring him any comfort. He certainly hadn't earned it from her. Dora took a few steps away from the dismal scene, then stopped. Her shoulders hunched up to her ears then dropped as she heaved a huge sigh. With gritted teeth, Dora stubbed out her cigarette and turned around. She shook her head, disbelieving of what she was about to do, and once more leant over her garden wall.
"Hey!" she called out to the brooding creature across the way. Dora heard Sherman sigh into his hands.
"Leave me alone, Debbie!" he mumbled just loud enough for Dora to hear him.

Sherman sat grumbling alone on the doorstep, his icy palms were cold and metallic against his face. He had heard Dora yelling over to him, and he hoped that he had done enough to deter her. With a stab of dread in his gut, he heard the gentle *crunch-crunch* of the gravel in his driveway. Reluctantly, Sherman peeled his face from his hands and looked up. Lo and behold, looming above him, was Dora. There she stood, in all her muddy-dungareed glory, clutching a giant woven basket of fruit to her chest.
Sherman snarled, "Oh, so glad to see you're back, Daisy -"
"*Dora!*"
Sherman rolled his eyes, "Whatever. Listen I'm *terribly busy* -"

He was cut short by suddenly having to fend off Dora's advances, as she tried to force the basket of fruit into his arms.

"I don't know what is going on with you, but a fruit basket will fix most things!" Dora insisted as she pushed the bounty of goods into his arms, "Everything in the basket was grown in our very own soil!"

Sherman breathed out through clenched teeth. For one thing, one of the items in the fruit basket was a pineapple, so clearly the girl was lying straight to his face. Furthermore, the apples and berries that made up the bulk of the offering were as large and glossy as though cast in wax. Sherman bit the inside of his lip as he finally accepted the basket. He leapt to his feet, as rigidly and monstrously as an ancient vampiric Count. Without a hint of remorse and with one fluid flick of his wrist, Sherman tipped all the fruit onto the ground.

Dora's jaw dropped open wide enough to inhale any one of the many apples that rolled along the gravel.
A vast shadow enveloped her as Sherman leaned over, his coat billowing out behind him like the glossy wings of an enormous bat. Dora's heart punched up into her throat and her feet impulsively carried her back a few steps. Her instinct had been right. She shouldn't have come back to this place at all.

Sherman bent down from his great height to stare Dora straight in the eye. His lips trembled as he fought off an outward growl. Eerily, Sherman's nostrils twitched as he took in a few unsettling sniffs.

"You smell like an ashtray," Sherman whispered, in disgust, "Don't you have any self-respect?"

Dora's eyes popped so wide they almost rolled out of her head. In a flurry of coattails, Sherman stole himself away and slammed shut the door.

Dora could say nothing. All she could do was ponder on the curious sentence that had been left with her.

****

Dora sat down wearily at her bedroom vanity table and gazed at her reflection. She couldn't help but wonder over the last thing that Sherman had said to her, and she sighed with confusion and fatigue. Dora pulled the tight bobble from her hair and absentmindedly reached towards her pot of hairbrushes. When her hand grasped empty air, Dora glanced sharply towards the pot with a grimace. Her favourite hairbrush was nowhere to be seen.

"Oh, bloody hell! Where've I put it?" she grumbled as she dropped to the ground to search for the missing brush.

Dora was blissfully unaware that only next door, Sherman was sat shivering upon the kitchen floor of the cottage. His knees ached as he knelt on the hard floor, craning over the small ceramic pot of red liquid. His palms were slick with sweat as he examined the large flat hairbrush in his hands. With trembling fingers, he pulled from its plastic teeth, a matted clod of thick purple hair.

****

The night of the full moon was finally upon him.
This was it.
Everything that Sherman had been working for.
It was time to act.
There was simply no room for error.

Sherman waited in the darkness inside his cottage, trembling as he stood at the front door, his hand shaking as he reached for the handle. Clutched in trembling fingers and tucked out of sight behind his back, was a giant serrated kitchen knife. His trip outside would have to be quick and efficient.
Sherman knew from his various reconnaissance missions that

getting into Dora's back garden could be done in silence and secrecy.

Sherman's lungs rattled like dice between his ribs as his hand tightened on the door handle.
It was time to go.
In one swift jerk, he wrenched open the door.
He nearly hit the ceiling in shock when he suddenly came face to face with Dora.
"What the hell?" Sherman shrieked, nearly tripping over in shock.

Dora smiled back, pleasantly.
She was simply waiting on the doorstep. In the dark.
Completely alone.

Dora looked up into his face and smiled.
"Oh hiya!" she said, pleasantly. Sherman's breath was barbed wire in his throat, and he spluttered as he tried to remain calm. His whole body filled the doorway as he stood there, unsure of how to proceed. His eyes were glossy and white as pearls as they threatened to roll back into his head.
"D…*Donna*…D…" he spluttered, uselessly.

Dora didn't bother to correct him. All she did was shuffle impatiently on the spot as she waited for Sherman to snap out of his trance. Finally, with one hand still wedged behind his back, Sherman pinched his brow with his free hand and breathed, heavily.
"Donna…" he forced himself to say, "What are you doing out so late? All by yourself too!"

Dora swallowed hard but smiled, "Look, I know we've got off on a really bad foot and I know it's late, but I just really needed to come speak to you!"

Sherman could barely hear her words over the pounding of his own heart.

"Can I just come in and have a chat?" Dora continued, earnestly, "I promise I won't bother you even one more time after this. I just want us to get some things straight, ok? I just want you to enjoy your time here and I can't help but feel like I'm ruining it for you,"

Sweat had begun to pour from Sherman's brow. Dora seemed so vulnerable, so small, as she stood there before him, swamped in a huge dressing gown that was the same shade of purple as her hair.

Dora's eyes flicked nervously back and forth as she wilted beneath Sherman's unhinged gaze.
"Uhh, Sherman?" she coaxed, "You alright there, hun?"
Sherman choked.
"Yes… umm… of course! Come in!"
Dora drew back in shock.
"Really?" she smiled, nervously, "Cool, I made muffins! I'll go get -"
"*No!*" Sherman barked, panic rising inside him. Dora shrunk back as Sherman's free hand came shooting out towards her and ushered her through the door. Tense beneath his touch, Dora allowed herself to be guided into the dark hallway.
"Y'know, there's a light switch right here?" Dora commented as she began to fumble blindly along the wall to her left. In her searching, she was too preoccupied to hear the click-clack of the door being locked behind her.

Dora's fingers finally brushed over the switch and light flooded the cottage. Pleased with herself, Dora clapped her hands together and took a few steps forward, only for her legs to become iron. The light around her seemed suddenly dimmer. Spindly wisps of shadow danced across the low wooden beams of the small cottage and Dora knew that she had made a terrible mistake.
"Oh shit," Dora whispered.

Ahead in the living room, Dora saw that one of her favourite coffee tables had been dragged over to the dormant fireplace.

It had been meticulously positioned inside a ring of blood red candles that were yet to be lit into life. A fine selection of metal handcuffs and leather straps were bolted to each leg of the coffee table.

The whole occult construction was watched over by the haunted, hollow gaze of a huge scrimshawed ram skull that hung over the fireplace.

An eternity crawled by in the time that Dora took to turn around. Her legs were trapped in the cement of time, as she turned back towards the door. There was nowhere for her to go. Sherman's vast form hung back in the hallway, blocking her path to freedom. Only the whites of his eyes sliced through the darkness as his monstrous form stretched to its full size, pressing his back to the door.

Dora's eyes flicked down and caught the glint of silver that was clutched in Sherman's trembling hand.

Dora took a step back.

Sherman took a step forward.

There came a chattering sound. Dora thought that maybe it was her teeth. Maybe it was Sherman's. Perhaps it was the very bones that rattled inside each of them. Still, Dora was unsure. All she knew for a fact was that Sherman's shadowy form was closing in.

"Sherman… sweety?" Dora trembled, "Whatever this is – you just let me leave. Ok? And we can just pretend that nothing happened, sound good?"

Sherman shook his head, stiffly. Tears gleamed bright in his pearly eyes as his mouth flapped open.

"I… I have to…" he mumbled, hoarsely.

Invasive vines of panic, white in colour and hot to the touch, crept up Sherman's throat as he prowled towards his hapless victim. Those vines very well could have sprouted from his mouth.

Especially when Dora started to laugh.

Sherman's skin prickled, aflame with dread. He recoiled, horrified.

Dora couldn't help herself. She had fought so hard to keep the smile from her face, but she had finally cracked. Her laughter exploded from her mouth and soon she was completely creased, her gleeful cackling bouncing through the cottage like ball bearings.
"Eeeeh well!" she laughed, slapping her knee in delight, "If this isn't just the most astronomical coincidence, I don't know what is!"

Sherman's stomach became lead.
"*What?*" he barked, as Dora peeled back her dressing gown and whipped out a giant wooden rolling pin from within its folds. It was all Sherman could do not to stumble backwards in panic as Dora bounced forward, and in one graceful swing, bludgeoned him in the left kneecap with her rolling pin.

Sherman's leg snapped backwards with a substantial, woody crack. His knee folded the wrong way at the joint, forcing his shin out ahead of him at a ninety-degree angle. Sherman crumbled to the ground, screaming as he went, and Dora made sure to kick the knife out of his hands.

"We got him, everyone!" Dora yelled at the top of her lungs. Giddily, she unlocked the front door and leant out over the step. As Sherman lay on the ground, wheezing and fighting against the growing shock, he felt as a flurry of hands grabbed him. Shadows massed around him and before he could fight against it, a sash was tied around his eyes to blind him.
"No!" he screamed in protest as he felt himself being lifted high into the air by many, strong hands.

A joyous chorus set up around him. A song of many voices and tones swam through the cold night air and soon, Sherman felt himself being lowered onto a hard, wooden surface. He fought with all he had to free himself but the pain in his leg was astounding, and the strength of those that held him was too much to break. His arms were forcefully spread out into a T-shape and were lashed in place to the wooden board beneath him.

"Let me go!" he screeched, fire climbing in his throat, "Let me go! Somebody *help*! Help!"

"Oh shush, silly, stop your fretting!" came a familiar voice as the sash was pulled from Sherman's eyes. He gasped as Dora's unyielding smile loomed above him. Sherman glanced around in a frenzy. He was out in the middle of a grassy field. A vast sea of joyous faces watched with glee at his unfolding predicament. The entire village had come out to witness the event; many of them were brandishing large wooden torches, aglow with orange flame.

Overhead, claiming the sky as her own with her radiant corona of ivory light, was the full moon.

"What the hell is this?" Sherman hollered, thrashing against his bonds, "Let me go!"

"You shouldn't be so cross, Sherman!" Dora beamed, "You're going to kick off our village fete for us!"

"What do you mean?" Sherman wheezed. The pain, once confined to his leg, had now morphed into an indistinguishable orgy of agony that raged through his entire body.

Dora took her place beside Sherman's feet and turned to address the gathered crowd. Promptly, a flaming torch was pressed into her hand by Tom the shopkeeper.

"Thanks, sweety," Dora smiled as Tom ducked back into the crowd. He gave a polite nod then stood in silence, obedient amongst his fellow villagers. Dora twirled her flaming torch for the pure drama of it, and the flames billowed around her like a hellish cape. She grinned maniacally and extended a welcoming arm to her audience.

"My dearest clan!" she addressed the amassed crowd, "As always, I have provided the key for our bountiful harvest.

And as always, there will be drinks and a barbeque afterwards back at my place!"
The crowd gave an appreciative cheer.
"Also, if we could give Mable a round of applause for her wonderful craft table!"
Dora's elderly neighbour, Mable, stepped forth from the crowd and gave a small wave. The sea of villagers cheered for her contribution and Mable blushed as she smiled.
"Just to let you know, I'll be drawing the raffle after the barbeque, so I hope you've all got tickets!"
"Pound a strip if anyone still wants a go!" Tom added, helpfully.

Dora waved a hand and the crowd fell to a compliant silence.
"Please!" Sherman choked, "I'll do whatever you want! Just please let me go!"
The crowd gave a collective chuckle. Sherman's skin blistered as every hair on his body stood on end.
"Sherman, hun," Dora began, "You've already done everything we could have possibly asked of you,"
Sherman's breath rushed to him in ragged, panicked convulsions.
"What?" he just about managed to get out.
"Yes, you see, we needed someone just like you!" Dora explained with a grin, "We needed a man who would come here of his own free will! A man who thrice refused an offer of kindness -"
"A man who shed the blood of our own!" Tom the shopkeeper chimed from his place in the crowd.
"A man who was a virgin!" Mable yelled, beside him.

There was an awkward pause. Dora pursed her lips and rounded on her neighbour.
"No Mable, wrong ritual," Dora added, curtly. Mable threw her hands to the sky and rolled her eyes.
"Well, when you've done as many as I have, you lose track!"
Tom leant towards her and gave her a quick, "*Shush!*"
Mable grumbled and stepped back into the crowd. Content with the silence, Dora marched confidently to the head of

Sherman's table where she stooped down to whisper in his ear.

Sherman was sure that he was close to losing consciousness. His brow was slick with sweat and his raven curls of hair stuck fast to his skin. He felt the heat of Dora's breath in his ear, though it did nothing to warm him. Not even the flaming torch that flickered so close to his skin could offer him any heat. Only the cold was there to catch him as he fell further into the icy madness. Sherman shook his head.

"Dora, please!" he whispered, "Dora, I swear I won't tell anyone what's happened here. Just let me go, please!"

Dora laughed, "Oh *now* you remember my name? I'm proud of you!"

"Dora please!" Sherman urged as Dora pressed her lips closer to his ear.

"Listen," Dora whispered, pouring an icy wave of panic down Sherman's back, "And I really mean this. Thank you for what you're about to do for us tonight!"

"Dora! *Wait!*"

"Bring the lid!" Dora ordered as she stood bolt upright and marched back towards the crowd.

"Dora no!" Sherman screamed though his pleas went unanswered.

From out of the assembled villagers, barged three large men. They were the Carter brothers; farmers that lived a few doors down from Dora. She had a special place for them in her heart, as whenever the lambing season came around, they would let her bottle feed the new-borns. Between them, the brothers carried a wooden covering, large enough to fit over a human body and hollowed out into a T-shape.

"Cover him!" Dora called. The men moved forward to obey her.

"No!" Sherman shrieked as he thrashed uselessly against his bonds. A shroud of darkness descended upon him as the wooden covering was slid over his body. No more did the moon hang in the sky above him. The sky instead was wooden.

Sherman howled in terror. His shrill calls bounced against his unyielding wooden prison and the sound was amplified tenfold in his ears. Still, he noticed amid his franticness, a small amount of light found its way to his eyes. He also realised that upon his hands and feet, still blew the cool breeze of the night air. They hadn't been covered by the wooden lid and had instead been left totally exposed. "You know what to do boys!" he heard Dora yell, and he once more felt himself being lifted into the air.

Dora stood back and proudly watched as the Carter brothers lashed ropes to each appendage of Sherman's craft table. Easily, they tugged at their respective ropes and lifted the makeshift casket off the ground.
"Lower him!" Dora commanded. The brothers complied without hesitation and carried their cargo over to a large open pit in the earth. Dora had dug it out with her bare hands only a few days prior and she was very pleased with her handy work. She watched the shaking casket as it shook and squealed, fighting against the ropes in the hands of the Carter brothers, a living wooden creature.

Sherman could feel himself being moved. He squealed and bucked against his bonds, though only succeeded in smashing his face against the wooden lid overhead. Blood poured back down his throat and he choked like a dying car engine. He suddenly felt himself being lowered and he heard the creak of straining rope. A wet cold touched his hands, lathering his exposed skin with loose clods of what must have been mud. "Jesus Christ!" Sherman wailed, "Please, please don't do this!"
Something rattled above him. A gentle pitter-patter against the wooden lid of his coffin. A hot, searing, stabbing breath caught in Sherman's chest as the sound made sudden, sobering sense.

Dora could barely hear the frantic screaming anymore. Her faithful followers had long since burst into song. Their joyful chorus drowned out the continuous howls of terror as the Carter brothers shovelled the loose dirt back into the pit, covering Sherman's casket with soil.

Hand in hand, the villagers sang together. The moon overhead smiled down at them and Dora gazed lovingly at the many faces that surrounded her.
All singing. All smiling. All together.

Dora glanced over to the Carter brothers who were now smoothing down the disturbed soil with their shovels, laughing amongst themselves as they did so.
"All done here!" shouted Ned, the eldest of the three, giving Dora a thumbs-up. Dora broke hands with her congregation and clapped. Soon, the whole crowd had erupted into a raucous round of applause.

The air inside Sherman's coffin was solid. Thick and hot as soup, it poured down his neck and into his lungs. He knew he would soon run out of air entirely. That didn't stop him from screaming.

He couldn't stop. Some wild, panicking beast lived inside him. Sherman could feel as it climbed up his throat and spewed out its wild shrieking terror like vomit. His hands and feet were numb with blue cold, crushed by the six feet of dirt piled upon them. The soupy air began to congeal inside him, and cold claws hooked painfully into his turbulently beating heart.

No one knew he was there. Absolutely no one. He had told no one about his trip.
No one would come for him.
He was going to die in that pit.
Still he screamed.

****

The muffled screaming sill raged on, but Dora and her
followers had once more burst into song.

"Right, everyone!" Dora yelled over the chorus, "Back to
mine for drinks and burgers!"

There was another communal cheer which quickly dissolved
back into song. En masse, the crowd followed Dora as she
trekked down the small hill that led back into the village,
leaving the screaming patch of earth in her wake. With one
final glance back, Dora noticed a small black shape sat upon
the pile of disturbed earth. Mittens the cat sat contently,
grooming herself as if unfazed by the muffled screaming of
her previous owner far below her. Dora chuckled. It was
always nice to acquire a new familiar.

****

A year had passed, and Dora once more had found herself
crouched in her front garden, tending to a patch of newly
sprouted daffodils. A little way ahead of her, nestled happily
under a rose bush, was Mittens the cat. The small animal
purred as she languished in the shade.

Dora clapped her hands free of the dirt that clung to her
palms and looked up to find Mable leaning over the garden
wall. The elderly neighbour wore a bright smile as she
proudly clutched a large wicker basket that was filled to the
brim with giant ripe bananas.

"This is the third time this year that banana tree has fruited!"
Mable yelled, "This year has been wonderful! Excellent job as
always, thank you Dora!"

Dora clutched a hand to her heart, grateful of her neighbour's
comments, then jumped to her feet and crossed towards her.

Before she could say anything further, a large four by four
came roaring down the small dirt road. It shrieked to a halt as
it pulled up into the driveway of the holiday cottage next
door. Dora gave a knowing smile as a man in a brown jacket
jumped out of the vehicle. He immediately bolted to the front
door of the cottage and allowed himself entry, using the key
that he had found beneath the doormat. Dora rubbed her

hands together in excitement as she excused herself from Mable.

Dora knocked firmly on the door and waited a solid few minutes before it finally opened to her. Lurking in the hallway, cast in shadow by the low ceilings, was her new guest.

"What?" he barked.

"Charles, is it?"

The man in the doorway raised an eyebrow and scowled. "How do you know that?"

Dora looped her thumbs in the straps of her dungarees and smiled.

"I'm Dora, the property owner. We spoke on the phone, remember?"

"Oh, is that you? I was expecting someone older,"

"I wouldn't worry, so do most people!"

"Oh, I'm not worried," Charles assured her, "Now please leave me alone. I'd like to get to work as soon as possible!"

"Don't you want me to show you around the house? There's a tap in the kitchen that doesn't quite…"

"Goodbye Dora!" Charles barked and slammed shut the door.

Dora waited a moment on the doorstep, giving Charles a final chance to open the door and change his fortune. No such thing happened, and Dora chuckled to herself as she left the garden.

"Strike one, Charles," she whispered, "Strike one,"

Dora would soon have another trench to dig. It wasn't a task that she begrudged, no not one bit. After all, it was within a person's basic needs to be covered in the soft soothing moisture of the earth. Mud was a must in Dora's life.

The fate of her village depended on it.

THE BEST BOY

Tony edged his car cautiously into the narrow cul-de-sac and pulled into his driveway with a sigh of relief. It had been a painfully slow drive home. An orchestra of car horns had been the musical score of his entire journey. The mounting queue of angry drivers behind him certainly had maintained a perfect and consistent symphony.

Tony paid them no heed. He was in too much of a good mood. In fact, he was in such high spirits that he hadn't even noticed that the mud-stained transit van of his neighbour Steve, was once again parked in the street's turning circle. The road was only just large enough for a single car to pass at any given time. Therefore, on any other day, this would have been perfect grounds for war. In truth, the van's placement had no direct impact on Tony's life. It was just that sometimes the thrill of neighbourly conflict was all that one needed to get them through the day. Not today though.

After all, Tony was carrying precious cargo. He glanced to the large cardboard box in the back seat, which had been poked through with four large air holes. Soft high-pitched snores emanated from the box's interior, and for a moment, Tony truly believed that his shrivelled heart would explode out of his chest into a rainbow- coloured pool of viscera.

Thankfully, he managed to collect himself just in time and no such aortal detonation occurred.

Tony skipped giddily up to his front door, box in arm, as he bustled his way into his house.

"Chief?" he yelled as he stumbled into the hallway and closed the door behind him, "Chief, come here, I've got a surprise for you!"

Tony made his way into the kitchen and placed the cardboard box down on the ground. He heard the sudden pitter-patter of paws clattering down the stairs and he turned to find his dog, Chief, loitering in the hallway.

"Come here boy, have a look in the box!"

Chief was a grizzled old German Shepherd with a muzzle full of scars and a chip in his left ear. His interest in that box was *limited* at best. It was only that he didn't want to dampen Tony's glowing enthusiasm, and so he decided to at least humour him. Chief sloped begrudgingly towards the box and nudged it. There came a sudden high-pitched yelp from within, and Chief snarled at the sudden disturbance.

"*Chief!*" Tony reprimanded as he pushed the enormous old dog out of the way, "That's no way to treat the new baby!"

Chief cocked his head and whined in confusion, as Tony pulled back the loose lid of the box to reach inside. Tony beamed with excitement as he pulled out a tiny wriggling puppy.

"Say *hello* to Trixie!" Tony exclaimed.

Trixie was the same breed of dog as Chief. Her youth, however, permitted her soft fuzzy ears to flop over into her eyes, and for her plush downy coat to stand on end as though she had just been for a quick spin through the tumble drier. She squirmed around in Tony's arms to better reach his face, then planted small dog kisses on his cheek with her tiny pink tongue.

"Aww, the *baby*! Aww, who's the baby?" Tony cooed as he ruffled up the pup's soft ears with his free hand. Chief was unflinching and moreover unimpressed. He rolled his eyes as he watched his master bounce the small pup in his arms and seemingly speak to her in tongues.

Oblivious to Chief's concerns, Tony was truly living his best life. He placed the puppy down on the ground and encouraged her towards Chief with a gentle nudge.
"Trixie meet Chief. Our grumpy old man in residence."
Trixie plopped down onto her haunches and stared up at the monstrous dog in total adoration. Chief made no move to greet her and instead gave a quick scornful grumble.

"Right, I'm going to get the rest of the stuff in from the car," Tony announced, then pointed an accusing finger towards Chief, "Chief, be nice to the baby!"
Chief huffed as Tony left them both in the kitchen to get acquainted. The old dog waited to hear the front door click shut, then glanced down to assess his new housemate.
The pup was chasing her tail.
With an eager yowl, Trixie lost her balance and flopped over onto her side.

"So, you're the new recruit, huh?" Chief growled, disapprovingly. Trixie rolled over onto her back and whipped her soft tail back and forth like a windscreen wiper. She gazed up at the huge brutish dog as though he was some Aztec idol come to life.
"The *Tall* says I'm called Trixie," the young pup yipped, happily.
Chief grunted, "That *Tall* is called Tony. He is our master."
"Tony?" Trixie repeated, testing the word out in her mouth, "Well, I've only met him today, but I think I love him more than anything in the world! Do you love him?"

Chief grumbled once more at her insolence.
"I protect him," he replied, sombrely, "He is very weak. And his teeth are blunt and useless.

Speaking of *useless…*"

Chief realised that Trixie was no longer listening. She had shimmied around behind him and was chewing on his tail, growling playfully. Chief collected himself with a sigh.

"I suppose if you're going to be living here, I better show you around. Come on."

Chief set off at a slow trot and dragged Trixie along in his wake when she refused to let go of his tail. He brought her out into the garden where she released him immediately in favour of exploring this new jungle. She bounded around on the grass in high spirits and periodically tripped over her own giant paws, landing in a fuzzy heap.

Chief growled, "This is where we come when we need to *go*. It's also perfect for lying down in silence and minding our own business."

His words fell on deaf ears. Instead of paying attention, Trixie ran in doughnuts through Chief's legs. Chief let out a guttural growl of annoyance, but it did nothing to deter the smaller dog's enthusiasm.

"We're gonna be best friends, Chief!" Trixie howled as she went. Chief squeezed shut his eyes and huffed loudly through his nose.

It was a sharp rattling that brought him back into the moment. He opened his eyes to find Tony leaning out of the patio doors. He was shaking a box of dog treats.

"*What's this then,* guys? Look what I've got for you!" he called in a silly, high-pitched baby voice that Chief had never been a fan of.

Chief had heard Tony speak to other *Talls,* but never once had he spoken to them in such a fashion. Trixie, meanwhile, had been infected by Tony's ever-spreading enthusiasm. She barked playfully and ran around in a circle.

"Trixie," Chief growled to grab her attention, "When Tony shakes the box, you go to him. It means he has food. Come on."

Chief padded over to his master and sat patiently. Tony
rummaged around inside the box and pulled out a small
bone-shaped treat.

"Good boy, Chief! *Paw!*"

Chief rolled his eyes but presented his paw. Tony shook it
once quickly and then held out the treat in compensation.

"You're my best boy, Chief!" Tony beamed as the old dog
took the treat gently from his hand and chomped it down in
one bite.

Tony pulled out another treat and waved it in front of Trixie's
soft muzzle. She leapt up and tried to snatch it from his hand,
but Tony closed his fist and pulled the treat out of reach.

"No, Trixie. Sit!" he said, firmly. Trixie cocked her head and
squealed in bewilderment.

"Sit, Trixie," Tony repeated. Trixie glanced across at Chief
for assistance.

"Listen to him. He wants you to sit down." Chief growled.
He was trying his *paw* at an *encouraging* tone, but he really only
succeeded in threatening the youngster.

Trixie whined again, "Why?"

Chief sighed, "No one knows. Sit down and give him your
paw. Then he'll give you the treat."

Trixie wheezed, confused, but did as she was told.

"Ooooh, what a good girl!" Tony fussed over her and
rewarded her with the biscuit. Trixie took it gently from his
hand and carried it away onto the grass, favouring playing
with it rather than eating it.

Chief glanced up at his master and let out an exasperated
whine. Tony glanced down in sympathy, knowing full well
what the old dog was trying to tell him.

"She'll be good for you, mate!" Tony assured him, patting
him on the top of the head, "God knows you could do with
some positivity in your life. It's not all doom and gloom, you
know?"

Chief huffed loudly as Tony turned to head back inside, leaving him alone to deal with the endlessly energetic puppy.

****

"Does Chief have to be in here?" Sam asked, nervously. Tony cracked open another beer and handed it to his friend.
"Yeah, he lives here," Tony snapped, "He's not bothering anyone!"
"He's bothering *me*! You know that dog scares the crap out of me!"

Sam had been Tony's best friend since University. They visited each other every third weekend to play video games and catch up over a few beers. Unfortunately, Chief's addition to the household had given Sam cause to rethink these visits, and he now preferred to hold the meetups at his place. This had been the first time in months that Sam had summoned the courage to step foot inside Tony's house.

Chief was sat a few feet away from his master. The huge dog was silent and still, as he stared vigilantly at Sam. Sam tried to ignore Chief's piercing glare by trying to focus instead on his game. His attempts were fruitless.
"Tony, can you put Chief outside?" Sam hollered, suddenly, and Chief let out a soft warning growl.
Tony shot his friend an offended glare.
"Will you leave him alone? He's just minding his own business!"
"No, he isn't, he wants to eat me! Can you just put him outside?"

Tony gritted his teeth in frustration but relented with a sigh. He paused the game and set down his controller, crossing the living room to quickly push open the glass patio doors.
"Sorry Chief, you're scaring the guest." Tony motioned with an open palm out into the garden. Chief huffed and trotted over to Tony's side. He shot one final glare in Sam's direction then padded out into the garden.

"Sorry, boy," Tony whispered, sadly, as he clicked the patio door shut. Undeterred, Chief took up his vigil once more and sat down before the glass. He stared into the living room, unmoving, never once tearing his eyes away from Sam. It was just then that he saw Trixie come tumbling into the living room. She had tripped over a large squeaky duck that she had been dragging along in her wake.

"Oh my God!" Sam exclaimed as Trixie came rolling across the carpet, "Can I pet her?"
"Yeah, go for it, she loves cuddles." Tony called as he left the room to fetch more beers. Sam pursed his lips and whistled to the tiny dog, who without need for further prompting, gleefully bounded over to him. Trixie rocked back on her hind legs and wagged her tail as Sam stroked under her chin.
"I have no idea who you are!" Chief heard Trixie bark, "But we should be friends!"

Chief narrowed his eyes and curled his lip. Just as he did so, Tony reappeared in the living room doorway. He hurriedly crossed the room and swept Trixie up into his arms.
"Do me a favour – go keep the big man company ok?" he said as he opened the patio door and dropped the puppy down at Chief's side.
"Go play you two!" Tony instructed, then closed the door. Trixie glanced up at the huge dog beside her and wagged her tail.
"Well, you heard him, you have to come play with me!"
"I have to do no such thing," Chief growled, without looking at her, "Now leave me be, I'm busy."
Trixie pouted and gave a small yowl of impatience, "You're not doing anything!"
"I'm keeping an eye on things," Chief grumbled.

Trixie glanced up and followed his eye line, coming to the realisation that he was staring at the other *Tall* that was in the living room.

"They're absolutely fine in there, Chief," she assured the old dog.

"I know they are. Because I'm keeping an eye on things," Chief responded in a low bark.

Trixie was sceptical. The *Talls* were fine, even though they seemed to be playing on what must have been some incredibly boring game. Not once had they got up and chased each other. Trixie wasn't actually sure how *Talls* had any fun together. But if Tony was happy then she was happy. She just needed to get Chief on board somehow.

****

Tony snatched up his controller and slammed himself down into his gaming chair.

"What's your problem, man?" he snapped at Sam, "Chief's settling in so well, why are you so weird about him?"

Sam shot him a glare as though he had just been addressed with some vile obscenity, "Because a dog like that has definitely killed people!"

"Well, yeah probably!" Tony mumbled, disheartened, "But he's a house pet now and he's doing a great job!"

Tony hated being at odds with Sam. These days, Sam was really Tony's only positive source of human interaction. Tony worked from home. Other than the hours that he allotted to walking the dogs, he had little time to stray from his desk.

The only social life that he really clung to, was that of regularly baiting his neighbours into a turf war. It certainly wasn't the exact life plan that he had laid out for himself. His parents were sadly no longer with him, and after the breakdown of a long-distance, romantic relationship, Tony had found himself orphaned and single. It really wasn't the highlife that he had planned in his mind's eye all those years ago.

****

Trixie had remained at Chief's side, not fully understanding the point of their endless watch. She had managed to hold her tongue for at least three minutes, but then grew too curious to contain her thoughts inside her tiny body.
"Answer me honestly. What do you think will happen if you stop watching them?" she asked, leaning over and nibbling Chief softly on the shoulder. Chief was unflinching.
"Hey, tell you what," he said, calmly, "You like games, right?"
Trixie bowed down and playfully jumped around in a circle.
"Yep!" she yipped.
Chief curled his lip and growled, "Good, then I've got a game for you. It's called '*far, far away*'. You should play *far, far away*!"
Trixie snorted loudly and flashed her tiny needle teeth in anger.

"Have you always been this miserable?" she sneered, though the credibility of her wrath was weakened when one of her soft ears flopped over into her eye. Chief's chipped ear twitched.
"If I was miserable, you'd know about it," he replied, coldly, "I'm just well trained, unlike some of us."
He shot Trixie a reproachful look, and she gawked back in disbelief.
"Tony trained you to be this *boring?*" Trixie gasped. She surely hoped that Tony didn't have the same plans for her.

Chief rolled his eyes and replied, "My *first Tall* trained me."
Trixie wrinkled her nose, as she struggled to think of any reason that a dog would need to swap *Talls*. The curiosity that filled her was overwhelming, but even the most inquisitive of pups knew to quit while they were ahead. Despite Chief's casual and unfeeling attitude, Trixie could feel the tangible sense of unease that rose like heat from his body.
Trixie settled on one last question.
"Do you miss your old *Tall?*"

Chief's brow knitted and he finally looked down at the young pup. Her small face was so innocent as she gazed up at him with her huge inquisitive eyes. Chief looked away again, as a distantly familiar face floated into his mind; a feather caught in the pastel Autumn winds of his memory. That face belonged to a *Tall* named Holly, though the other *Talls* would always call her Ma'am. She was strong, like him. Her mind was sharp, and she thirsted for adventure. Chief would follow her every command. He remembered how his heart was lifted into song whenever her bright smile rewarded his bravery.

But their world was a cruel one. A world far away beyond the sea, where the burning sand bit into his paws and stung his eyes. A place where the breeze carried with it the piercing, unrelenting screams of distant anguish.

Chief decided to ignore Trixie's question. Thankfully, she didn't ask again.

****

"One more round?" Tony asked as he crushed his empty beer can in his fist.

"Nah, mate. Sarah's on her way now. She wants to get home before it starts absolutely pouring."

"A bit of rain never hurt anyone," Tony replied, a little disgruntled.

Sam scoffed, "Yeah, well if you didn't live under a rock, you'd know that there's a weather warning out for tonight. And if you don't mind, I'd prefer to not get caught in it."

It wasn't long after that that Sam was collected by his fiancée, Sarah. As Tony hung out of the front door to bid the couple farewell, the heavens opened. It was with a violent flash of fork lightning that the rain announced its arrival. It poured in unrelenting sheets, as though tipped from an enormous celestial bucket. Tony gave a final wave to his friends. He watched them reverse out of the narrow cul-de-sac, then he slammed shut the front door.

Tony bolted through the house and into the front room to let the dogs back in from the garden. Trixie had squashed her whole face up against the glass as she waited forlornly to be allowed back inside. Her fur was already soaked through. "Aww poor baby, I'm sorry!" Tony called as he wrenched open the patio door. What had once been a fluffy puppy was now little more than a soaking rodent, as she bounded inside. Trixie shook the rain from her fur and sprayed brown water all over the walls and furniture. Tony was oblivious to the mess. He was too busy trying to coax Chief inside.

"Chief, come on boy!" he yelled, though his requests were ignored. Chief was sat on his haunches. He was staring straight up into the sky, growling softly at the torrential downpour.
Trixie noticed too.
"Chief? It's just rain!" she barked to him, "Come inside, you'll get sick!"
Chief didn't let up.
"No," he muttered, suspiciously, "Something's coming."

It took a while for Tony to lure Chief inside. Even when the old dog had relented, he glued himself to Tony's side, and followed him around the house like a clingy child. Trixie, meanwhile, was scampering around the house and busying herself with her squeaky duck toy, oblivious to Chief's disquiet pacing.

After having tripped over Chief for maybe the fourth time, Tony finally lost his patience.
"What's up, bud? Can't you just chill out?" he snapped. The old hound dropped down onto his haunches and gave a high-pitched imploring whine. Tony sighed but dropped down to sit cross-legged on the floor.
"Come here you muppet!" he called, his arms outstretched. Chief's ears twitched. Tony whistled.

With a reluctant groan, Chief padded over to his master and pressed himself into his open arms.

"Who's my best boy?" Tony cooed as he smushed the huge dog's face into his own and kissed him on the snout. Chief gave a low, apathetic grunt. He was indifferent to Tony's overly sentimental attitude. However, he was perfectly willing to be fussed over and molly-coddled for his master's sake. Tony pulled back and smiled as he squished Chief's face gently in his hands.
"Right, calm down and go to sleep!" he commanded, then headed upstairs to his bedroom. Chief trotted up the stairs after him and sat down on the landing, just outside the bedroom door.

It was a narrow, rectangular landing with a large bay window at one end. The perfect sun trap around noon. Chief would sometimes lie in the warm spot that it created on the carpet.

Tony gave Chief a final scratch behind the ears.
"Night, you mad dog," he said, as he stepped inside his bedroom and closed the door. Chief let out a low whine, then lay down and curled up into a ball.

Maybe he *was* just overreacting. After all, he'd had many sleepless nights worrying over an imminent attack, only to rise in the morning to nothing more than a bowl of kibble and a pat on the head.

Chief had just allowed his eyes to slide shut, when Trixie came bounding clumsily up the stairs and pounced on him.
"Have you stopped worrying yet?" she asked as she clambered over his back.
Chief grumbled, "I am never worried, I am simply alert!"
Trixie scrambled over his head then fell awkwardly into his outstretched forepaws. She rolled onto her back and smiled up at him.
"Well, are you finished being alert?" she chuckled. Chief flashed his fangs at the insolent pup, and she yelped in shock.

"Wow - alright, ok!" Trixie groaned, indignantly, "You know, you really need to lighten up? Tell you what. We'll wake up really early in the morning and dig a massive hole in the garden!"

"That's a solid *no*!" Chief barked.

"Well, you can pick what we do then!" Trixie barked, irate at his lack of enthusiasm. She would have rattled off some more suggestions, but all she could manage was a high-pitched, squeaky yawn.

"We can decide tomorrow," Trixie yielded, as she curled up into a ball on top of Chief's paws.

"Night, Chief," she mumbled.

Chief flattened back his ears, unimpressed. He lay his head on top of Trixie, and gave an indifferent grumble, "Good night, pup."

"Love you!"

"Good *night*, Trixie."

****

Trixie awoke in the middle of the night, cold and alone. She sleepily lifted her head and glanced down the landing. Her sleepy daze melted away in an instant when she saw the distinct, bristling silhouette of Chief, as he stood between her and the large bay window. He was silent and unmoving, as he stared out into the darkness. Trixie flattened her body as low to the ground as possible and slunk over to Chief's side.

"What's wrong?" she whispered.

Chief didn't look at her.

He answered, barely moving his lips, "There's something out there."

Chief had barely spoken, when the whole window flooded with an ethereal, piercing white light, that engulfed them in a tsunami of neon.

Both dogs set up barking at the intrusive light. Their primal baying echoed across the narrow landing in an anarchic war cry. Chief had devolved into a nightmarish shadow beast. An ocean of foam frothed at his gnashing jaws, and his eyes glowed an unearthly silver. Even Trixie was unrecognisable. What had only moments ago been a sweet fluffy pup, was now a wiry, feral hound of the night.

The slithering eel of dread in Trixie's gut had whipped its tail and transformed into convulsing electrical coils of pure terror. At that point, Trixie didn't even know where her fears truly lay. All she knew was that something unspeakable lurked beyond the window, within that otherworldly light. There was a sudden clattering from behind them, as Tony wrenched open his bedroom door, and loomed in the doorway like a phantom.

Tony stepped out onto the landing and yelled, "What the hell do you think you're barking at? It's 4 am!"
He squinted and raised a hand to shield his eyes from the piercing light. He was confused, though too dazed by the ungodly hour of the day to comprehend the gravity of the situation. Both dogs ceased their barking and turned to their master with a pleading whimper.

Trixie galloped to Tony's side and yowled in warning. Tony bent down and easily scooped the little dog up into his arms. He bounced her gently as he tried to halt her cries. He was too busy trying to quiet his howling hounds to notice that the intense glowing light had dimmed to complete darkness.

Suddenly, the entire window exploded in a tempest of raining glass. Tony screeched and recoiled to shield Trixie from the storm. His bare back took a lathering from the biting glass and blood poured down his skin like wet paint.

Chief squeezed shut his eyes and braced through the pain. When he opened them again, the intrusive otherworldly light was once again shining bright. Lurking in its ominous glow, was an enormous, writhing shadow.

Tony risked a glance toward the intruder. He couldn't help the animalistic wail of fear that escaped him. The shadow slithered through the window, as fluid as water, and poured itself onto the landing before them.

It was enormous. So huge was it, that the rippling arches of its back brushed easily against the ceiling. Its serpentine body was black and slick with scales, and its tapered arrow-shaped head hung low on a long, slender neck. Four solid, crusty legs jutted out high from its back, each one having to snap down at a severe angle to reach the ground. The creature flicked a forked tongue and flaunted its mouthful of sheer silver fangs.

In a flash, it folded its spidery legs flat to its body and launched itself down the landing.
All four of Chief's paws left the ground as he lunged at the oncoming, slithering monster.

The two beasts collided hard. A boulder smashing into a mountainside.
The incredible impact knocked the squirming creature off balance, and it toppled to the ground like a crumbling monument. Chief went straight for the exposed throat, though not fast enough.
The monster's flailing tail curled over and smashed into the old dog, hurling him easily against the wall. Chief yelped on impact and slid to the ground.

The creature turned its attention to Tony, who clutched Trixie closer to his chest in fear. Trixie flashed her tiny needle teeth and she bristled like a ball of wire wool. She knew full well that she was horribly outmatched, but she would die before that slithering abomination laid a single scale on Tony.

The monster flicked its tongue and moved in. Its armoured legs had only taken a single step when Chief sprung up beside it, and body-slammed it into the wall. The wall crumbled beneath the monster's weight and it tumbled through into the spare room. Chief didn't waste a second. He pounced over the wreck of the crumbled drywall and landed atop the writhing animal. He galloped over its stomach towards its fleshy exposed neck. This time, Chief didn't miss. He sank his fangs deep into the creature's throat. Blood gushed from the beast's torn jugular, as though sprayed from a fire hose, and splattered up the walls like the gaudy artwork of a disobedient child.

The creature's panicked squeals soon became wet gurgles, as it flapped and bucked, desperately trying to free itself from Chief's iron grip. It soon stopped struggling and Chief felt the dead weight hanging from his jaws. He released his prize and leapt back through the wall into the landing. Tony was frozen in place, but Trixie was squirming frantically in his arms.
"Chief!" she yowled, "Are you ok?"
The huge dog growled, "Of course I'm ok. Now come on, we need to move."

Tony was still staring at the devastation in the hallway but came to his senses with a sharp bark from Chief.
"Jesus Christ!" was all Tony managed to say. He could hear the chorus of screams and sirens outside. He forced himself to the end of the landing, wary of the felled beast, and looked out of the window. He could see people fleeing in all directions. Abandoned cars were jack-knifed across the narrow road, clear evidence of failed panic-fuelled escape attempts. Tony's stomach lurched as he saw that his own car had been crushed and wedged against a wall by a familiar mud-stained transit van. He looked between his two dogs and gave a ragged, panicked sigh.
"Right, come on!" he managed to say. He nipped back into his bedroom, Trixie still in arm, and grabbed his phone from his nightstand. He shoved on some clothes then shepherded his whole crew downstairs. Tony flung open the door to his basement and hurried down the creaking steps with Chief close at his heels.

Tony placed Trixie down on the cold stone floor and began to fumble hurriedly with his phone. Trixie was straight to Chief's side and she began fussing over him with worry. "Are you alright?" she asked as she gave him an all-over sniff to check for injuries. Chief was bleeding a small amount from above his eye. Trixie rocked back on her hind legs and tried to helpfully lick the wound, but Chief shrugged her away. "I've told you I'm fine," he snapped, "We have bigger problems."
The two dogs glanced to their master, who was frantically smashing his phone's keypad.

By that point, Tony had called the emergency services several times, but they were ringing off the hook. He had only one other person to call. He dialled the last number in his call history and held the phone to his ear. Tony held his breath as he waited. Eventually, his call was answered.

"Tony?" yelled Sam's voice through the speaker.
"Oh, thank God!" Tony gasped, clapping a hand to his chest, "Sam what's going on? Are you alright?"
"We're driving out of town, mate! Our home's gone! Destroyed! Something … something came in…"
"Listen, Sam," Tony cut him off, "My car's wrecked! I'm stuck here, please… I need your help!"
"Are you being *bloody* serious?" Sam's voice was little more than a prolonged wheeze of dread.

There were muffled voices from the phone line, and Tony knew that an argument had broken out between Sam and his fiancé. Tony knew that *he* was the source of the argument. They were arguing over whether or not to save his life.
 "Right," Sam's voice came back through the phone, "Hang tight, we're coming to get you!"
Sam had already hung up before Tony could say anything further.

Tony then spent the next two minutes flying around the house, throwing essentials into a dusty old backpack. Once done, he snatched Trixie up from the ground and whistled Chief to his side. They waited silently at the front door. Tony knew that the road outside was impassable by car. There was no way Sam would be able to get close enough to his house. They would have to run for it.

Tony counted to three.

He held his breath and wrenched open the front door.

In flooded the frenzied screams of Tony's panicked neighbours. He watched as they shoved and jostled one another; many were barged straight to the ground and trampled in the commotion. People scrambled frantically over the many wrecked cars, only to be unceremoniously dragged to the ground by others with the same idea. There was a sudden piercing shriek from above and Tony looked up. He realised in terror that another serpentine creature was prowling along the street's rooftops.

The scaly animal sat down on its haunches, poised gracefully like a panther upon an elevated throne. But with the pulsing throng of panicked citizens, the creature was spoiled for choice. To commit to a single target upon this rolling smorgasbord seemed like a waste. The strange beast's perusing was cut short when a second reptilian creature came skulking over the rooftop beside it.

This one was less choosy. It leapt from its rooftop perch and landed amid the frantic masses. The shrill screams climbed ever higher, as the creature snaked among the crowd like a shark through a shoal of fish. A significant portion of the crowd abandoned their escape attempts and made a beeline to the shelter of their own homes. The first creature took advantage of this new wave of panic and also leapt down from the rooftop.

Tony didn't want to see the outcome. He hugged Trixie tightly and shot out of the door. The crowd had thinned enough for him to roll clumsily over the many wrecked car bonnets without fear of being kicked to the ground. Chief cleared each one easily in a single bound. They left the cul-de-sac, and the three of them made a break for it into the main road.

The sudden screech of rubber caught them off guard, and the trio was swallowed by the headlights of a fast-approaching car. The driver had slammed on the brakes, but it was too late.

There was a visceral crack, as the car ploughed into Tony's hip. His legs caved beneath him and his body folded over the car bonnet like a napkin. He rolled onto the ground and landed in a crumpled heap. The collision had knocked Trixie from his arms, and she skittered hard across the tarmac. Chief yelped in horror and galloped to the fallen pup, snatching her up in his jaws.

"I'm ok," Trixie yelled, as she hung from the old dog's mouth, "Go get Tony!"

Chief spun on a paw and bolted back to his fallen master. Tony was struggling to scramble to his feet, but he consistently sunk back to the hard ground with each attempt. The car door swung open and out jumped Sam.

"Jesus, mate! I'm sorry!" he hollered, as he skirted around the car to his fallen friend.

"Sam?" Tony managed to mumble. Sam hauled Tony's arm over his shoulder and dragged him to the car. He fumbled with the back passenger door and folded Tony inside.

"Get… dogs…" Tony muttered, barely conscious. Chief padded towards the vehicle, but Sam had already jumped into the driver's seat and slammed shut the door.

"You're not bringing the damn dogs!" Sam yelled, and the car roared into life. Sam floored it and off the car sped. It screeched away and quickly disappeared into the chaos of the night.

Both dogs were stunned into complete silence.
Their one lifeline in this madness had been severed.

They were alone.

Chief realised that he wasn't breathing. For a few moments more, he remained that way. In all his life, after all he had seen, he had never been so stunned. He couldn't feel his own body. There was nothing inside him but a cold numbness, as he stared unblinking down the long highway.

"He's gonna come back, right?" Trixie managed to say, "He'll come back for us, right Chief?"

Chief had heard her, but his keen ears also told him that the pandemonium was not isolated to their street. The whole town for miles around was alive with terror. The dogs needed to find cover. Chief tightened his jaws around Trixie and trotted briskly back into the cul-de-sac. He carried her back into their home and through the swinging door of the basement. The door clicked shut behind them and there they stayed.

****

Chief poked his head out of the front door and scoped out the street. Dawn had broken. A soft layer of mist had risen from the many dew-laden lawns to coat the morning in a wash of grey. All was silent. Chief had initially thought this to be a blessed relief from the harrowing sounds that had rumbled on mercilessly through the long night. But now as he waited in the complete ghostly silence, he wasn't so sure.

Chief waited a while longer just to be safe. His nose and ears told him that there were no immediate threats, but there was certainly no harm in being cautious.

"Is there anything out there?" came Trixie's voice from behind him. Chief's eyes scanned the street a final time.

"No," he concluded, sternly, "Let's go."

Every house in the cul-de-sac had suffered gravely. Walls had been caved in, windows had been smashed to smithereens, and doors had been knocked clean from the hinges. Trixie took a deep sniff of the air and her stomach turned. She whimpered and felt as her body flattened nervously to the ground.

"Everyone's dead," she whispered.

She was right.

The overwhelming stench of death was as tangible and acrid as the thick clogging smoke of burning rubber. Both dogs knew that if they ventured too close to any of the exposed houses, their paths would be littered with the bloody remains of what had once been their neighbours.

"Let's go," was all Chief had to say.

Just like their cul-de-sac, so too had the next road received its fair share of battle scars. Houses were damaged beyond recognition; vehicles had been left abandoned in the road and the smell of death hung ever-present in the air.

For a while, neither dog spoke to one another. The only sound that marked their journey was the crunching of gravel beneath their paws. Trixie was starting to flag but she knew she couldn't stop. Tony was out there somewhere. Just like Chief had said to her, *'Talls* are weak and need us to protect them.'

Trixie shivered at the thought of Tony facing one of those monsters on his own. That sudden image panicked her enough to make her yelp and jump up as though she'd trodden on something sharp. Chief swung his head around and scolded her with a snarl.

"Quiet! Do you want those things to come back?" Chief hissed through bared fangs. Trixie shook her head but could no longer contain her fears.

"How are we going to find Tony?" she whimpered, and tucked her tail between her legs, "We have no clue where he went! And he's out there somewhere without us! What if he's hurt? What if he's … dead?"

Chief shrugged off her concern.

"Tony is not dead. Also, we do know that he went *this* way," Chief jerked his head in the direction of their travels, "We carry on until we pick up his scent. In silence, preferably."

The old dog trotted on at quite the pace but halted abruptly when he realised that his tiny shadow had fallen away from his side. He spun quickly and gave a low growl of frustration. "Pup, we *absolutely* do not have time for this right now! You need to be strong. If you lag behind again, I'll *leave* you behind…"

His aggression melted slightly when he realised the state of his tiny cohort. Trixie had dropped down onto her haunches, her head hung low, her ears flopped over her eyes. She was sniffling softly to herself, and small pitiful whimpers seeped from her trembling leathery lips.

Shockingly, of all the many wonderful skills that Chief had learned from his time in the field, comforting crying puppies was not one of them.
"Stop crying!" he barked sternly, confident that this first attempt would be successful. It was not.

Chief growled again and Trixie sniffled in response,
"I'm not crying."
"Then act like it and let's go!" Chief grumbled. Trixie sighed wearily and slowly lifted her eyes to meet Chief's piercing glare.
"I'm really trying to be strong and brave. Just like you! But I can't fight those monsters! I can't… I *couldn't* protect Tony from them! And now he's out there without us, facing who knows what kind of horrors! What kind of dog am I if I can't protect my *Tall?*"

The reproachful snarl slowly dissolved from Chief's lips. He gave a long relenting sigh and trotted over to the pup to sit beside her.
He leant down and spoke softly into her ear, "I would be lying if I said that you weren't very small and weak. You

definitely are very small and weak. But what you lack in size, you make up for in spirit."

He took a deep breath as he prepared himself for the weight that he was about to shift from his chest.

"I'm going to tell you something that you'll find surprising. And if you ever repeat this to anyone, I'll bite your head off."

Trixie lifted her head and listened.

Chief began, "In truth… and honestly, this shocks me… I wish I was more like you."

Trixie's ears pricked up, and her tail gave the smallest of wags.

"Really?" she asked, in disbelief, "Why?"

Chief sighed, "I admire your outlook. Every day is an adventure for you. The smallest most insignificant things fill you with joy - a joy that you spread to others just by being in the room. Me on the other hand? I have to leave so as not to frighten the guests."

Trixie couldn't believe what she was hearing.

"But you're so brave and strong!" she exclaimed. Chief shook his head.

"Bravery and strength aren't always about being the biggest, meanest dog in the street. Sometimes, courage is like having a tapeworm – a small thing can soon go a long way."

Trixie knitted her brow at the comment.

"Now come on – your insufferable whining is giving me a headache," Chief barked, as he jumped to his feet, and headed out. Trixie sat for a moment longer and pondered over the older dog's admission. She realised quickly that her tail had started wagging, and with a blithe roll of her eyes, she trotted after him.

After a good long trek, in silence of course, the pair found themselves in the town centre. Chief had been here on several occasions when Tony had brought him along to run errands. Today, it was unrecognisable. The town was void of all life. A haze of smoke hung in the air, as the two dogs crept through the dusty ruins of the once thriving hub. Their hackles bristled with unease.

Both of their noses had been clogged with the bitter sting of smoke, but for a brief moment, a new scent blew in their direction. Chief's ears and tail pricked up as he listened closely.

"Are you getting this?" Chief whispered.

Trixie nodded eagerly, "Yeah! *Talls*!"

The pair took off at a gallop. They shot nimbly over the many hills of rubble and weaved easily through the columns of toppled concrete. They came up over a lip of debris and gazed over the ledge into a vast concrete crater. They were greeted with a welcome sight, when they found two male *Talls* loitering far below them at the bottom of the pit. Both were clad from head to toe in green camo, and each was armed with one of the long metal fish that *Talls* called guns. Chief was very familiar with this branch of *Tall*. He knew that they referred to each other as *Soldier*.

Though he couldn't place why, Chief's elation suddenly gave way to an icy wave of dread. An inexplicable feeling, he just knew that something was off. Trixie had no such reservations. Her tail wagged furiously, and she began to bark in excitement.

The *Talls* in the crater were clearly startled. They glanced up sharply and regarded both dogs with an expression of blatant fear. They then began to discuss something amongst themselves, making sure to keep a wary eye on both dogs. "*Everything? Right?*" Chief heard one of them ask. The other nodded. The first soldier shook his head despairingly and turned his gun towards the still barking Trixie.

"Damn shame," he muttered as he took aim.

Chief's heart dropped into his gut like a rock cast into the ocean, as he immediately realised what was happening.

"Trixie!" he barked, as he snatched the puppy up into his jaws. Trixie yelped in shock as her feet left the ground, and she hung from Chief's mouth like an old sock.

Chief turned tail and skidded down the mountain of rubble. The roar of gunfire rumbled behind him, spurring Chief's paws to thunder ever faster across the ground. He heard the sudden rattle of sliding rubble and instantly knew that the soldiers had given chase.
Chief didn't look back. He just needed to find cover.

Trixie bounced roughly in Chief's jaws, but she certainly didn't argue. Neither did she make a peep when he threw her into a large earthy fox den beneath a fallen concrete slab. Trixie weaselled her way deeper into the den and Chief raked over the loose rubble with his paws to conceal the entrance.

The dogs were thankful to have been spared from complete darkness. A gap beneath the concrete slab that sheltered them, allowed for a small ray of sunlight to seep inside.
Trixie's back tingled and her fur stood on end.
"Chief, look!" she whispered in panic. The soft ray of sunlight was suddenly doused into darkness by a large shadow. The two dogs hardly dared breathe as they heard two voices outside.

"Did you hit them?" they heard one of the voices ask.
"I think so." came the other.
"You *think* so?" berated the first voice, "You need to be sure! Orders were to *shoot anything that moves*!"
"Ok then, I'm sure!" snapped the other voice, followed by an incoherent, irritated mumble.
"I just don't get it!" the same voice started up again, "What kind of operation are they running over there if their systems are gonna fail under one tiny storm? I mean yeah, if one or two got loose... but all of them? *Really*?"
"We're not here to question, we're just here to clean up the mess."

Trixie's eyes shot wide open. Her already bristling hackles stood even higher on end; her skin burning beneath the prickling sting of adrenaline. She slunk as far back from the concrete slab as possible.

"Chief," she hissed, suddenly petrified, "There's something else out there!"

Chief flattened his whole body to the ground and stifled the growl that was building inside him.

"I know," he said.

Just as he had spoken, the panicked yelling began. Outside of the dogs' small stony sanctuary, anarchy had been given a free reign. The thunderous gunfire rattled Chief and Trixie's sensitive ears. Guttural, unearthly roars rose even higher over the deafening tolls of unloading shells, and the frantic yelling soon gave way to piercing, pleading screams. Within a matter of minutes, the chaos outside fell into a complete and eerie silence. The fox den was hot and clammy with the adrenaline-filled panting of the two dogs. They shared a panicked glance as the sound of heavy, unnatural footfalls moved towards their hideaway. The sound was suddenly above them. The dogs could hear as vast lungs were filled with heavy huffs of breath. There was another thud and suddenly, the heavy breathing was right outside the concealed den entrance. Both dogs held their breath. There was a snuffling and a sudden scratching at the dirt.

They were being dug out.

In an instant, sunlight flooded the den. A flash of gleaming silver claws sliced through the dirt and unearthed the dogs from their refuge. A colossal beastly head the size of a bear's, pushed through the entrance, jaws wide open and jagged as a Venus flytrap. Its skeletal, bleeding jaws were studded with bright sabre fangs. Soulless, crimson eyes rolled back into its head. The den shook with monstrous roars and rumbling canine snarls as the enormous creature pushed its way deeper inside. Chief bounced forward to meet the monster head-on, narrowly dodging its gnashing jaws.

The dog sank his fangs deep into the beast's exposed nose. The creature shrieked. It retracted its massive head from the burrow, dragging Chief along with it. Trixie yelped in horror and darted along after them. She emerged above ground and was immediately pounded in the face by the coppery scent of blood.

Chief was grappling with the monster. He had thrown the creature's balance and had rammed it to the ground, where it lay on its side, thrashing and bucking as it violently struggled to defend its long neck. Chief wrestled hard to stay on top of the creature; snapping and snarling, foaming at the mouth as he desperately fought to silence the giant writhing animal.

In the harsh sunlight, Trixie could finally see the monster in all its horrifying glory. It was as large as a carthorse, but as bald and fleshy as a lab mouse. Its limbs seemed uncannily long for its body, and huge seeping boils bubbled across its skin like melted cheese.

A thick cloud of ash and dust had been kicked up in the fracas, and Chief was struggling to keep his eyes on his target. The creature seized the chance and swiped up a clawful of coarse dust into Chief's face.
Chief's eyes burned, and he couldn't help but instinctively squeeze them shut. It was all the distraction that the creature needed. It clobbered Chief hard in the ribs and sent him flying through the air.
"Chief!" Trixie screeched as she bolted into the fray. She had no idea how she was going to help, but she would be damned if she didn't do something.

Chief landed hard in the rubble and lay there, stunned and winded.
Trixie was straight in. The creature jumped to its feet and swung around its massive head, right as Trixie ran onto it. The monster idly swiped at the small pup, expecting to easily swat her away. Trixie was much too nimble. The tiny dog ducked easily beneath the blow and slid under the beast's

massive body. She rocked back on her hind legs, and with all the might she could muster, plunged her needle teeth into the monster's soft underbelly.

The creature squealed and reeled up like a bronco. Trixie didn't let up. She knew her teeth were small, but they were certainly sharp. The creature creased over and made a desperate grab to dislodge her. In the moment it took to extend its fleshy arm, Chief had come flying across the rubble and launched himself headlong at the monster like a bottle rocket. This time, the huge dog hit his mark. He plunged his fangs into the beast's throat.

Its rancid flesh burst open as easily as a ripe banana skin between Chief's crushing jaws. Blood gushed across the ground in an abstract crimson splatter. Wet gurgles bubbled from the creatures severed throat and its ungainly legs crumbled beneath its hulking body.

Trixie bolted out from under the monster before its falling mass could crush her, and Chief was waiting to snatch her up in his jaws.
He carried the pup over a lip of concrete and left the dying animal far behind them. He didn't stop running until he was sure he could no longer hear its death cries.

****

The pair had slowly and carefully made their way to the very outskirts of town, narrowly avoiding several encounters with the many grotesque beasts that now roamed the streets. Both dogs were very conscious of the wind direction. The path they were travelling placed them upwind of any nightmarish creatures that may have lay ahead. They had encountered many other abandoned pets on their travels, but they hadn't stuck around long enough to get acquainted.

Trixie and Chief had found themselves on a trail in the bottom of a rubble valley, with sheer banks of shale to either side of them. The road ahead sloped up and led to a narrow pass where two walls had collapsed into one another. They would have to shimmy through one at a time.

"Chief?" Trixie piped up, "How do we know we're still going the right way? We haven't even got Tony's scent." Chief gave a low growl of annoyance, "Because I can hear him."
Trixie was taken aback by this.
She tilted her head and gave a small, confused whine, "You can *hear* him?"
"Of course, can't you?" Chief replied without looking at her, "He's yelling our names."

Trixie squeezed shut her eyes and listened intently. Her hearing was just as good as Chief's, but there was nothing to be heard over the crunch of gravel beneath her paws. If there was a voice out there to be heard, especially that of her beloved *Tall*, she would have heard it.
"Chief… I can't…"
"You can't *what?*" Chief swung around and flashed his fangs, making Trixie yelp as she leapt back in shock.
Trixie had been growled at plenty of times before, but never once had she taken it seriously. This time was different. As Chief stood there before her, caked in blood and dust, his jaws dripping with foam, it was the first time that Trixie had ever been afraid of him.

A sudden clatter of disturbed rubble distracted them. Both dogs turned towards the sound and a low bark came from atop the hill before them. Trixie wagged her tail in response.
"It's just another dog!" she exclaimed, in relief.
Chief bristled warily and called out to the hidden intruder, "Show yourself!"

Out crept an auburn furred Irish setter. He was limping badly and one of his silken ears was torn and shredded. He stumbled through the rubble and blocked the narrow pass with his body.

"I don't recognise either of you," the Setter muttered. His voice was enough to cease Trixie's wagging tail. Instead, every hair on her body stood high on end. The Setter's voice was wholly unnatural. It seemed oddly distant, and gave off a low mechanical buzz, as though he was the speaker at the end of some long-distance phone call.

Chief didn't flinch.

"We've never met," he assured the other dog, "Maybe we should pretend like that is still the case and go our separate ways?"

The Setter seemed undeterred and was bold enough to take a step closer.

"If we have not met, then you are not one of us. And that is very peculiar indeed."

In subconscious response, Chief had stepped over Trixie, and tucked her beneath him.

"What are you even doing out here?" the Setter asked in his metallic voice.

Trixie poked her head out warily from beneath Chief's chest and summoned the courage to speak.

"We're looking for our *Tall*," she replied, timidly.

The Setter curled his lip and snarled.

"*Talls* are filthy," he spat.

Trixie wrinkled her nose at the comment.

"No, they aren't," she assured the Setter, "They're our friends."

"Some friend, to leave you both to die out here," the Setter retorted, sharply.

"No!" Trixie insisted, "It was an accident. He didn't mean to…"

"Face it pup, your *Tall* doesn't want you," the Setter snarled, adamantly, "They're heartless! They have no regard for life or death. My whole life I've been one of their playthings. I've felt such indescribable pain and seen things that would be enough to drive your tiny mind to madness."

Trixie flashed her needle fangs.

"I don't believe you," she sneered.

"No?" quizzed the Setter, "Only yesterday I was strapped to a table, surrounded by *Talls*. They filled my veins with fire and waited for me to die, then applauded and congratulated each other when I didn't."

"*Talls* wouldn't do that!" Trixie protested.

"This is what they do!" the Setter scowled, "It soon wasn't enough that I had merely survived their torture. It was clear that they wanted more from me! With each blast of poison, the *Talls* grew more and more impatient… but then the storm came."

"You're lying!" Trixie cut in, once more, "Chief, he's lying right?"

But Chief couldn't respond to her. The Setter had clocked the sudden deep sadness in Chief's pained eyes, and his lips shrivelled back into a deranged grin.

"I know that look!" the Setter growled in his mechanical voice, "Those eyes have seen things that no living being should ever have had to see."

Trixie whimpered in confusion and glanced up.

"What does he mean, Chief?"

There was silence. Crawling shadowy memories scuttled through Chief's mind, like spiders dancing along a web, snaring him in their silk and dragging him back into their lair of nightmares.

Chief shook his whole body, wanting to shake himself free of this whole situation.

"Ignore him Trixie, he's sick."

He glanced back to the Setter and growled, "Now if you could kindly move, you're upsetting my puppy."

At this point, the Setter was completely unresponsive.

"Hey!" Chief barked, growing impatient with this nonsense, "Get out of the way!"

The Setter remained quiet and perfectly still, as he loomed above them in the narrow rocky pass. Chief had had enough. "Wait here," he whispered to Trixie, and made his way up the hill of rubble, grumbling as he went. He had just about made his way up to the brow of the hill when he stopped short.

The Setter was trembling. Buzzing, in fact. His skin and bright auburn fur oscillated as though he was hooked up to a power source.
"Hey?" Chief barked again, though now he was suddenly unsure of himself.

Stark red foam began to pour as freely as melted wax from the Setter's jaws. His eyes bulged from his skull and without warning, burst completely like crushed grapes, and seeped down his cheeks in a free flow of puss and viscous scarlet sludge.

Chief absolutely did not need any further prompting to get the hell out of there. He pushed hard with his forepaws and skittered backwards down the rubble hill. He saw as the Setter's fur dropped from his body in huge clods.
The Setter's newly exposed pink skin roiled and pulsed like plum tomatoes bubbling in a pot. Great oozing wounds tore open suddenly across the *once-dog's* back, and with an ethereal howl of anguish, creaking bony appendages, steaming hot and dripping red, burst through the Setter's skin.

Chief reached the bottom of the hill, snatched up Trixie in his jaws and bolted in the complete opposite direction to the monstrous mutation. However, in the commotion and chaos, he had neglected his other vital senses.
"Chief!" Trixie hollered as she bounced wildly in his jaws, "There's a ..."
She didn't get the chance to finish. It was too late. Chief knew it.

Waiting in silent ambush in the path ahead, lying flat on the ground, was an armed soldier. Chief skidded hard and took off up the sheer rubble hill to his left, just as the soldier unloaded his entire round. Chief didn't stop. He scrabbled manically up the sliding shale as the sky lit up behind him. He threw himself and Trixie over the brow of the bank but still, he did not stop. Chief bolted into the open doorway of a decimated convenience store and ducked behind the crumbling counter. He gently placed Trixie down on her feet. The pair panted heavily to catch their breath. They sank low to the ground and kept quiet as they listened to make sure that they hadn't been followed.

After some time, the pair slowly rose to their feet, and Chief cautiously peered around the edge of the counter. Trixie, who was glued to his side, suddenly felt as her stomach shrivelled into dried tripe.
"Chief?" she said, softly, "You're bleeding."
Chief didn't need to be reminded. He knew. He hadn't been quick enough.

Blood was pouring from the large fresh wound at his ribs and was pooling on the floor beneath him. He glanced into Trixie's wide panic-filled eyes.
"It's nothing, don't worry," he said, gruffly, then made his way to the exit door. He didn't get very far before his hind legs gave out beneath him, and he slumped down hard to the ground.

Trixie yelped and darted to his side. She licked his snout gently as she encouraged him to get to his feet. Chief panted, heavily. There was a new fire in his lungs with every breath, and creeping shadowy tendrils had begun to crawl in from the corners of his vision.
"Chief, please get up!" he heard Trixie beg - her voice seemed miles away.
Chief swung his head around to look at Trixie.
"I'm fine," he lied, "Now come on, let's go."
It took him all his strength to haul himself back onto his feet. He began the long, painful journey to leave the safety of the

convenience store, leaving a trail of crimson paw prints in his wake.

****

Thankfully, once outside, there was no sign of the mutated Irish Setter or the soldier. Perhaps they'd killed each other. Chief thought no more on it. It didn't matter anymore.

The two dogs had lost track of time; they had no idea how long they'd been padding along that dusty, winding road. Chief felt a sense of urgency like he'd never felt before. Every time he glanced down at Trixie trotting along beside him, his heart sank. He could feel his legs about to buckle beneath him once again when Trixie wedged her soft body against his, bracing him to remain upright.
"Come on, Chief," she implored him, "Please!"
He stopped for a moment and looked down at her.
When he had first been forced to meet her, she was a spoiled, obnoxiously loud, soppy little pup. But as he looked at her now, with all that fiery determination in her eyes, and fangs that had pierced the flesh of a monster, he could feel his old unfeeling heart swell with pride. It was for her that he so desperately wanted to continue. He truly did.

Chief took a few more determined steps, then collapsed.

"No, please!" Trixie begged as she threw her weight against him in hopes to budge him. Chief tried. He willed his legs to move, but he only succeeded in dragging himself along the ground a few inches. His body simply would not cooperate.
"Chief, *please*! Please get up!" Trixie beseeched him, her voice wavering in panic.
"I can't," Chief sighed. Trixie whimpered and curled up on the ground beside him. She licked his muzzle comfortingly.
"I'm so sorry, Trixie," Chief whispered, his voice hoarse and pained, "I didn't want any of this for you."
"It doesn't matter, Chief!" Trixie assured him, but he shook his head, weakly.

"I lied to you…" he wheezed, "I made you so many promises that I couldn't keep…"
"Chief, it's gonna be ok, we can still get through this!"

"You were right, you know?" Chief managed a soft chuckle; the situation absurd to him now, "I couldn't hear Tony's voice either. I never could. It was a cheap trick. I was just fooling myself,"
Trixie squeezed shut her eyes and pushed herself even closer to Chief, willing her strength into him. In the back of her mind, she fancied that she could hear Tony's voice echoing through the misty wasteland ahead.

"Chief? Trixie?" Tony's voice swirled around Trixie's mind, taunting her. He would have known how to help. He would have scooped Chief up in his arms and held him tight. Trixie whimpered.
"Chief? Trixie?" Tony's voice goaded her again. It seemed so close.
So real.
Very real.

Trixie's hair stood on end and her ears perked up to listen. Her breath caught in her throat. She narrowed her eyes in disbelief.
Staggering towards them through the thick mist, hunched over and propped up by a large makeshift cane, was the distinct lanky shadow of a *Tall*.
 "No, Chief," Trixie whispered as she stared longingly at the approaching silhouette, *"You weren't!"*

Chief didn't understand. With great effort, he dragged his head through the dirt and forced open his eyes. The figure ahead of them coughed loudly on the thick rock dust that hung in the air, then leant back and screamed into the sky, 'Chief! Trixie!"
Chief's heart glowed gold inside his chest. Just for a moment, the pain that wracked his body melted and gave way to a rolling wave of unrivalled glee.

The shadowy figure finally stumbled through the mist and emerged into full view, wheezing and crying as he came. He stopped a little way away from the two dogs and craned his neck forward, brow furrowed and eyes narrowed.
"Chief?" Tony whispered in total disbelief.
Chief's tail thumped wildly against the ground and his breath came to him and sharp, longing wheezes.

Tony was running to him now. Chief didn't know how, but somehow, he was also running. The pain had nothing further to take from him as he loped like a yearling towards his best friend. Trixie hung back and watched, tears stung her eyes and her tail wagged frantically as she beheld the glorious reunion.

Tony slid down to the ground and threw his arms wide open. Chief slammed hard into Tony's body and lavished his face with dog kisses.
"Who's my best boy?" Tony sobbed openly, as he squeezed Chief tight against him. The old dog's head was draped over Tony's shoulder and pressed up hard against his face.
"I was looking everywhere for you buddy!" Tony wept, "I never thought I'd see you again!"
As he said it, he realised that his hands were completely stained red.
He quickly located the pouring wound on Chief's side.
"Ohh… No!" he pleaded and Chief soon slumped down into Tony's lap.
 Tony leant forward and cradled him, kissing him softly on the head.
"You're my best boy," Tony wept, and Chief's tail wagged, weakly.

Trixie took a few steps forward but sat down and kept her distance. It wasn't her place to involve herself.
Chief glanced Trixie's way, and locked eyes with her, as he lay contently on Tony's lap. Chief wasn't afraid for her anymore.
He knew that if she grew up to be half the dog that she'd

already proved herself to be, she'd certainly survive whatever this new world would throw at her. Chief's tail flicked weakly as he gazed lovingly at the young pup.

Slowly and deliberately, Chief's eyes slid shut.

"Hey, pal." Chief heard a distantly familiar voice. He opened his eyes immediately, and noticed a wispy silhouette hanging back in the mist. It was the distinct, straight-backed figure of another *Tall*.

The *Tall* took a step forward, put her fingers to her mouth and whistled. Chief found himself drawn to the call, and before he could even comprehend how, he was on his feet and trotting towards her. Chief hadn't noticed that he was no longer shivering, or that the pain that had throbbed deep in his chest was no more. He sat at the *Tall's* feet and gazed up at her face. It was her smile that struck him first. A beautiful, glowing smile that lifted his old heart into song…
Chief wagged his tail.
No matter how many worlds apart they could ever have found themselves, Chief could never have forgotten that face. The face of his beautiful, adventure-loving, brave as a lioness, Holly.

She crouched down and ruffled Chief's ears.
"You're such a good boy, Chief," she said, proudly. Holly rose and turned on a heel to walk away. Chief went to follow her, but something made him stop. He glanced over his shoulder.

Behind him, he could see Tony. He was cross-legged on the ground, clutching tight to his chest the lifeless body of an old, battle-scarred dog. Tony's screams of anguish were muffled where he had buried his face in the dog's blood-stained fur. Trixie was sat beside them. Her head was laid softly atop the hound's cold body, her ears flattened back, and her eyes squeezed shut.

Chief's heart sank, but he felt a hand on his shoulder. He looked up and found Holly beside him, who responded with a warm smile.

"Don't worry about them," she said, calmly, "They'll be fine. You know they will."

Chief whined, concerned. He watched as Tony laid the old dog's body gently on the ground, and Trixie threw back her head and howled. Tony leant over and lifted Trixie into his arms and hugged her tightly.

Chief's heart ached for them, but deep down, he knew that Holly was right. Trixie and Tony would survive this. There was no way that they wouldn't. Chief knew it.

Holly gave another soft whistle.

Chief tore his eyes away from his friends but wagged his tail. He padded contently to Holly's side and licked her hand.

"You're the best boy," Holly said.

Together, side by side, they walked away, and melted into the mist.

TEEN DRAMA

"Chad is totally gonna ask me to the dance!" Kayla announced as she clutched her schoolbooks tight to her chest, like a toddler oblivious that its loving embrace was squeezing the life from the family cat. Marni scoffed as she struggled to keep pace with her friend down the long corridor.

"Chad is totally the coolest boy in school," Marni scolded, her face flushed red, "He only dates cheerleaders!" Kayla brushed off the comment with a wild, unhinged grin. "I have a plan, Marni! It's totally gonna work and by the end of the day he'll *have* to ask me to the dance! I just know it!" Marni opened her mouth to protest but her attempts were instantly thwarted when Kayla's hand slammed over her mouth.

"*Shush*, here comes Chad!" Kayla breathed, her eyes wide, "Be cool!"

Swaggering leisurely down the long hallway, a gentle breeze ruffling his golden hair, and light shimmering in eyes of pearlescent blue, was Chad Wilding.
The coolest boy in school.
 He was tall and muscular, a hulking golden lion in a blue varsity jacket. He smiled as he came, flashing teeth as bright and perfect as cut glass. Kayla was sure that wherever he went, the faint hum of soothing music followed him.

Chad sauntered slowly up to the girls and fired a slew of finger guns in greeting.
"Hey Kayla! Hey Marni!" Chad grinned. Kayla's face glowed as bright as a traffic cone and she cast her gaze to the ground. She mumbled a quick, "Hi Chad."
 Marni tutted. She held Chad in the same regard as being bitten on the eyelid by a disease-ridden rat.

Chad gave a carefree chuckle and sashayed on his way. Kayla held her breath until he had fully disappeared around a corner and out of sight. As soon as he was gone, Kayla's knees buckled, and she fell back hard against a wall. She slid to the ground in disbelief.
 "Did you see the way he *totally* just looked at me, Marni?" Kayla panted, fanning herself with one of her workbooks. Marni gave her an incredulous scowl, "He smiled at you. He was just being polite!"
Kayla rolled her eyes and ignored her friend. She considered Marni as close as a sister. But sometimes, as is often the case with sisters, Kayla could have quite happily strangled Marni to death with her bare hands.

Marni was completely useless as a wing-
woman. She considered herself to be above dating boys and simply had no time for them. She much preferred instead to focus on her schoolwork - art in particular - so was most comfortable in her baggy paint-covered overalls. Her jet-black hair was always scraped back into a ponytail, and her enormous thick-rimmed spectacles rested heavily on her slim nose.

Kayla was the chalk to Marni's cheese. Kayla's mousy blond hair was pulled up into high bunches, as it always was, so that she could more easily display whatever choker she had decided to wear that day. Today's piece was bright blue with a clear plastic love heart dangling from the front.

The pair had been making their way to the lunch hall before Chad's brief interruption. Marni knew that this had cost them valuable time. After all, the longer one spent out in the open no-man's land of the school corridors, the easier it was to run into unsavoury characters. All too easy indeed.

 Loitering beside the lockers, lying in wait like crocodiles in a watering hole, were the Conway sisters. The Conway sisters (not blood relations contrary to their name) were a trio of cheerleaders that one would be foolish to trifle with. They clung deftly to the highest rung of the social ladder and happily spat on those that clambered far below them. It was for that reason that Kayla and Marni fell very much into their line of fire. Especially today.

The leader of the trio, Erica Conway, was leaning back against a locker like an old-timey gangster ready to start a well-choreographed dance fight on the streets of New York. Flanking her like bodyguards were her two thugs, Laura and Charlotte.

Erica's face glowed with a devious grin when she spotted her new quarry. The cheerleader pushed herself away from her locker and stepped directly into Kayla and Marni's path. Laura and Charlotte skirted behind the pair and blocked off any possible escape route, trapping them in a circle of bodies. Erica smiled and blew a huge bubble of pink gum that she had been chewing with insufferable vigour. The gum was the same colour as her outfit – a tight-fitting vest top and skirt that clung to her soft marshmallowy skin like a candy wrapper. Even the fluffy hair ties that held her perfect blonde pigtails in place were the same garish pink.

Kayla was already intimidated. She could immediately see why boys found Erica irresistible. Marni, on the other hand, found Erica about as appealing as being offered sexual favours by a lobster.

"Don't think we *totally* didn't see you talking to Chad, earlier!" Erica snarled, snapping her fingers directly in Kayla's face, "You don't really think you have a chance with him, do you?" Kayla couldn't look the cheerleader in the eye. Instead, she found a spot on the floor to focus on. Marni grumbled and stepped up.

"Nothing to do with you, Erica!" she snapped.

"Oh, I think it is!" Erica grinned, wickedly, "You see, Chad will totally be going to the dance with me! Why would he want to be seen with losers like you guys?"

"We're not…" Kayla tried to speak up, but her nerves forced her to trail off.

"What's that?" Erica yelled, snapping her fingers once more in Kayla's face. Kayla had nothing further to contribute and bowed her head submissively to stare at the floor in silence. Erica chuckled, menacingly.

"That's totally what I thought!" she sneered then jerked her head, signalling her crew to follow. The two cronies barged passed Kayla and Marni with a smirk and took their place behind their leader.

"See you later losers!" Erica shouted over her shoulder and the trio trotted away down the corridor.

Kayla was fighting to hold back tears. Marni noticed immediately but for the sake of Kayla's pride, she drew no attention to it.

"Come on Kayla, let's go get some lunch!"

The pair pushed their way into the lunchroom and joined the queue to grab some food. They took their meals to a secluded table at the back of the hall and dug in.

"Hey, have you seen Taylor, recently?" Kayla asked, through a mouthful of her sandwich. Marni shrugged and shook her head.

"Not for a while. He must have transferred,"

Before they could discuss the matter further, they found that their focus had been drawn to the middle of the lunchroom.

There was a girl standing alone amid the tables.

Her eyes were wide and panicked as though she was trying to scope out the best escape route. Neither Kayla nor Marni had ever seen her before. The girl looked to be about fifteen – maybe sixteen at a push. Her slender body was swallowed by the folds of an ill-fitting black blazer, and a loose-knotted school tie lolled from her neck like a dead goose. Her gaudy yellow hair was scraped back into two boxer braids that were so tight they pulled back the skin of her already narrow face.

Kayla and Marni shared a glance and sighed. They each noted the uninterested faces of their fellow students around the lunch hall. The pair decided it best that they intervene.
"Hey, new kid!" Kayla yelled. The girl looked over to them in horror.
"Yeah, you!" Kayla assured her, waving her over, "Come sit with us!"
The new girl wandered over to them but did not take the seat that she had been offered. Instead, she remained standing, seemingly aware that she may have to suddenly flee.
"What's wrong, new kid?" Kayla asked, gently, as the girl stood looking dumbfounded before her.
Kayla tried an even softer tone, "You lost?"

The new girl scowled.
"Yeah, *chick*! I am bloody lost!" she spat in a thick, unrecognisable accent. Kayla drew back in confusion.
The new girl continued on her tirade, "I'll be honest with *yuz*, I *am* a bit confused! This morning, I rolled outta *me* own bed, in *me* own house, walked into school, as usual… and now I'm surrounded by Americans!"
Kayla and Marni shared a glance.
"Oh, so you're the new transfer student?" Marni leant forward and gave an exaggerated wink, "If you know what I mean…"

"What are you on about?" The new girl could have breathed fire, "Do you think I'm thick?"

"*Thick*? Uhh… No… not at all," Marni assured her, holding up her hands in a passive, calming gesture, "Hey look, why don't you start by telling us your name?"

New Girl grunted, "It's Becca!"

Kayla took in a deep breath and smiled, hopeful that Becca would now no longer erupt, "Ok and where are you from?"

Becca grunted again and replied, "England."

Kayla raised an eyebrow.

"You're… British?" she whispered, "How come you don't sound like… you know?"

Becca's left eye twitched.

"*What*?"

Kayla swallowed hard and she mumbled, nervously, "*The Queen*,"

Becca rocked back and crossed her arms.

"Yeah babes, well that's coz the Queen lives in London! You absolute *melt*! I'm from up *North*!"

Kayla wrung her hands together, anxiously.

"There's a North Britain?" she asked.

"Shut up, babes," Becca snarled.

Becca, by no means, was having a good day. One could even go as far as to say that she was having a terrible day. She had indeed walked from her own home, the same home in which she had lived her whole life, to the very same high school that she attended every weekday. Well, most weekdays.

Ok, *some* weekdays.

When she could be arsed. This had come to be a rather sore point between Becca and her mother; her mother very much being in favour of her daughter receiving a full education. A controversial opinion if Becca ever did hear one.

That very morning, Becca had left the house without saying goodbye, and made her way to school for the first time that week. It was a Wednesday. She had entered the school building at 9:05 am. Despite her tardiness, she had casually strolled through the building to her assigned form room for registration. However, on pushing open the door, she had not been greeted by her regular tutor group in their usual stuffy history classroom. Instead, she had found herself in a huge open-plan dining hall which was bustling with people that she had never seen before in her life. The door had closed and locked abruptly behind her and that is where she had stayed.

"Becca, *huh*?" Kayla reiterated, interrupting Becca's train of thought, "Well I'm Kayla and this is Marni!"
Marni gave a small acknowledging wave. Becca sat down at the table beside them and narrowed her eyes, suspiciously. She hated Kayla's voice for a start. It was high pitched and nasal. It seemed as though she was blowing all of her words through a kazoo. Becca stared on for a moment more and silently assessed the pair. There was something very odd about both of them.

"How old are *yuz* both?" Becca asked, her brow furrowed deep in concern. Kayla and Marni shared an impish giggle.
"We're sixteen," Kayla replied, proudly.
Becca shook her head in disbelief and curled her lip.
"*Yuz* clearly aren't!" she growled.

Becca was completely correct. There was no hiding it.
It was plain to see.
Kayla and Marni were both fully grown adult women.
Both of them.
Not teenagers.
Adults.

Becca speculated that they must have been nearly thirty years in age. Now that she thought of it…
Becca risked a glance around the vast lunchroom. Just as she suspected, the entire student populace was comprised of *grown-ass* adults.
Slowly, Becca turned back to face her new companions.
"Be honest with me babes, am I having a stroke?" she asked, listlessly, as though she could slip from consciousness at any

moment. Becca's question was never answered as Kayla had now elected to ignore her in favour of pointing across the hall.

Chad Wilding was making his way across the lunchroom.

"Be cool!" Kayla exclaimed, grabbing Marni around the shoulder in panic, "He's coming over! He's coming to talk to us!"

Becca turned in her seat for a better look. Making his way very, *very* slowly across the lunch hall was an enormous golden-haired jock. A football type - the kind of guy that Becca had seen in cheesy old movies.

Chad, Becca couldn't help but notice, was walking exceptionally slowly. On top of that, anyone who strayed within an arm's reach of him also slowed down to such a point that it seemed that their bodies were calcifying in his presence. Every smile Chad flashed - every finger gun he fired - was painfully slow. A sudden swell of cheesy pop music filled the lunchroom. It seemed to be emanating directly from Chad. It was playing perfectly in sync with his tedious footfalls. A sudden hiss of purple fog materialised from thin air, and Chad strolled confidently through the cloud, emerging dramatically on the other side as though he hadn't even noticed it. Becca's face drained completely of all colour.

"I'm in a nineties teen rom-com!" she muttered to herself, in absolute horror.

After about five minutes, Chad had finally made his way over to their table. Without being asked, he sat down in the remaining seat.

"Hey ladies!" he said - thankfully at a regular speed. Kayla grimaced with pure envy as Chad's eyes wandered over to Becca. Becca was less than pleased with the attention.

"Say, *new kid*," Chad purred as he placed a hand gently onto Becca's, "Why don't you and me head outta here? You could come and watch me play some football? I'm the best on the team!"

Becca snatched her hand away and snarled. Chad was also quite blatantly a fully grown, adult man. *Yes,* he was very muscular and handsome - very much Becca's type. On any other day, she would have actively pursued a guy like this. But today she had simply run out of patience.

"You're the best on the team, are you?" Becca asked, forcefully. Chad nodded and gave a bright smile.
"Is it because you're twenty-seven and built like a brick shit house?" Becca quipped. Chad drew back, sharply, as though he'd been stung.
"I've just turned sixteen!" he exclaimed, obviously wounded by her remark. Becca groaned and turned her palms to the sky, pleading to whichever deity may have been on hand to deliver her from this madness.
"Am I in a coma?" she yelled out, in anguish, "What the hell is going on?"
Her trio of tablemates shared a glance. Their eye contact could only have lasted a second at most, but it seemed heavy somehow; loaded with some hidden burden. Becca wrinkled her nose at their exchange.
They knew something that she didn't.

Before she could quiz them any further, Chad rose from his seat and fired some more finger guns in Becca's direction.
"I'll see you later, pretty girl," he grinned. As soon as he had spoken, the swell of pop music filled the room once more and Chad walked away. *Incredibly slowly.*

Becca turned sharply to the remaining girls and flashed her teeth like a dog.
"If someone doesn't tell me soon what the bloody hell is going on, I'll swing for *yuz* both!"
Kayla and Marni shared a shy glance then carried on as though they hadn't heard her.
"Chad likes you," Kayla announced, jealously, "but that gives me an idea!"
"What the *fu-*"

"You need to convince Chad to like me, new girl!" Kayla jumped in, swiftly, "You can help me out, right?"

"No, I can't help you, you absolute freak show!" Becca screeched, tossing back her head as though in the throes of transforming into a werewolf. She stood up from her seat and turned on a heel.

"See you later, you actual bunch of skets!" she sneered. Becca went to march away but only succeeded in taking one step. Instead, she froze still in her tracks.

There was a lunch table a little way ahead of her, occupied by a single person. As Becca stared, her skin blistered with an electrical crackle as though she had jammed an exposed finger into a plug socket. It was a man that sat there alone at that table – an older, balding man in a black turtleneck sweater. There was nothing special about him. No haunting, ghostly disfigurements brought about from the grave. No ghoulish halo shone from his eyes. Nothing. He was completely normal. So why was it that Becca's hair bristled like wire when she gazed at him? Why did a chill run down her spine when he glanced up and made direct eye contact?

Becca choked as she locked eyes with the man. A strange sense of familiarity washed over her. Though she had no idea why. She was sure she had never seen that man in her life. Or at least, she was pretty sure…

As the man in the turtleneck folded forward over the desk and massaged his face in his hands, exhausted, Becca was overcome with an unmistakable shiver of dread. Kayla shuffled nervously to Becca's side and she tapped her softly on the shoulder.

"You see him too, right?" Kayla whispered. Her voice was sincere, no longer was it the nasal, chirpy tones of a fake high schooler. It was the voice of a concerned adult woman. Becca nodded, her teeth chattering in her skull.

Suddenly, the man at the table sat rigid in his seat. He opened his mouth and out poured a rattling roar of frustration. He brought his fists crashing down hard against the table.
In a flash, the very world began to tremble around him. The chaos was instant and perilous. The entire lunchroom shook furiously as though caught in an earthquake. The walls and ceiling coughed out a cloud of dust as they quivered, terrified, beneath the man's fury.

Becca was sure that she was screaming, though she could hear nothing over the raucous quaking of the room around her. Kayla shot out a hand and grabbed Becca by the shoulder. She pulled her close and wrapped her arms around her, shielding Becca from the commotion. As the dust rained down, the man screamed again. This time the noise that left his mouth was inhuman. His voice was distant somehow; echoing and raw like the screams of one injured, alone and dying at the base of a canyon. Sharp black lines, jagged and coarse as the legs of a giant spider, burst from the tips of his fingers. In place of the haunted screams, the lunchroom instead filled with a vicious scratching sound, like paper being attacked with a blunt pencil. Just when Becca's ears could have burst from the rising cacophony, it was over.

As quick as that, all was silent. Becca hadn't noticed but she had squeezed shut her eyes from panic. As she dubiously opened them, she realized with a shudder that the man had disappeared from his table.
Vanished.
The lunch hall had dimmed to silence and all was still.

Slowly, Becca peeled herself away from Kayla and she stared around the lunch hall, trembling in every limb. Kayla pressed a gentle hand to Becca's shoulder once more and Becca turned around, her eyes glossy with tears.
"We should go," Kayla whispered, "Come on,"

Becca nodded slowly and allowed herself to be pulled away from the lunchroom.

****

Once in the hallway, Becca barged passed the other girls and slumped hard against the wall, fighting desperately to hold back tears.

"What the hell is going on?" she whispered to herself, her throat burning. Only last night had she been tucked away in the safety of her own home. She had stumbled through the front door at midnight, despite having been previously forbidden from leaving the house at all. She had fallen into the hallway, stinking of smoke and booze. An explosive argument had broken out shortly after, when Becca had found her mother sitting in the dining room waiting for her.

Becca's pity party was cut short when she realized that she had been dragged onto her feet. Kayla and Marni stood to either side of her, their arms linked with hers. Together, arm in arm, they set off down the long corridor. Becca was ruthlessly dragged along, like a sulking toddler that would have much preferred to have been carried.

"We can't stay here," Kayla whispered, cautiously into Becca's ear, "We have to keep moving."

Becca allowed herself to be pulled along. It was not in her nature to be passive, but right now she felt as though her body was not her own, as if she was sitting in a theatre stall, watching these maddening events play out before her.

As they turned a corner, another surge of generic, high-energy pop music rung out loudly. Three women came strolling down the hallway towards them.

Becca wasn't sure how much more of this she could take.

"Oh no, it's the Conway sisters," Kayla whispered in fear, readopting her nasal and falsely childish tone.

Becca gave a loud groan.

Easily Twisted

The Conway sisters strutted in time to the beat of the music, but periodically slowed almost to a halt for dramatic effect. The approaching cheerleaders were only a few feet down the hallway, but it took them a good five minutes to cover any ground. Especially with all the agonizingly slow hair flips that made them seem as though they were whipping their heads through a vat of treacle. Becca was on the verge of dropping to the ground and crying in frustration.

The Conway sisters eventually made up the distance and stopped right in front of Becca.
Erica Conway, the gang Don, leant in close.
"Don't think we *totally* didn't see you talking to Chad, new kid," Erica spat in contempt, "You should *totally* know that Chad only likes cool girls. And you are *not* a cool girl."
Becca looked Erica up and down and scoffed. The *very* limited vocabulary that this fully adult woman seemed to possess gave Becca a severe case of second-hand embarrassment. Becca squared up to the cheerleader and raised an eyebrow.
"Wow! You *really are* a loser!" Erica chuckled and tugged mockingly at one of Becca's braids. Becca pursed her lips and swatted away Erica's hand.

"Touch me again and I'll deck all of yuz!" Becca snarled at the head cheerleader. Erica backed up, shocked by the retort, then glanced back at her henchwomen for support. All they offered was a panicked shrug. Erica spun around in a flash and glowered like a rabid possum.
"You are like so *totally* rude!" Erica grimaced and rolled up her sleeves, ready to fight, "And we're *totally* gonna make you pay!"

Erica then began to dance aggressively.

She pushed her fists together in front of her chest, locked out her elbows and thrust her whole body, rapidly. Not once did she break eye contact with Becca, who was watching the whole ordeal in open-mouthed confusion. Erica continued to convulse as though she was very purposely trying to wrench her hips free of her spinal column. Without missing a beat, Laura and Charlotte Conway joined the war dance and fell into formation with their ringleader. At this point there wasn't even any mysteriously sourced background music. Their only accompanying soundtrack was the awkward squeaks of shoes against tiles and the sound of heavy breathing. Laura and Charlotte shimmied backwards, and each pulled out a pair of cheerleading pompoms from behind their backs. As they waved them in formation, a twirling baton materialized in Erica's hand.

They began to chant:
"WE ARE THE CONWAY SISTERS - AND WE RULE THIS SCHOOL.
NOBODY COMPARES TO US – WE'RE THE BEST – WE'RE COOL.
WE'RE THE COOLEST CHEERLEADERS - AND BOYS WANT US SO MUCH,
WE'RE TOTALLY AMAZING - WE HAVE THAT SPECIAL TOUCH!"

Becca had had enough. She had never heard such lazy lyrics or such blatant and offensive disregard for rhythm.
"I warned you," Becca growled. She cracked her knuckles and neck like a seasoned mobster, and before anyone could even think the words 'throat jab', she punched Erica square in the trachea.

Air exploded from the lead cheerleader's mouth in a tempestuous wheeze. Her hands flew up to clutch at her throat as she stood, wide-eyed and hissing like a furious goose.
Becca slugged her again right in the nose.
Blood spurted in a firework of scarlet sparks from Erica's face and she staggered back in a daze. Finally, broken and spluttering like a wrecked car, Erica dropped to her knees in defeat. Becca pounced on her wounded prey, nostrils flaring and eyes flaming, ready to finish the job. Before she could

land any further damage, Kayla swooped in. She dragged Becca away from Erica's twitching body and slammed her against the wall, pinning the teenager easily in place with the advantage of age and strength on her side.

"*Geroff me!*" Becca choked as she squirmed for freedom, though she soon ceased her struggles.
Becca's hair stood high on end and the air in her lungs solidified. The lights in the hallway gave an electrical sputter. They began to flicker sporadically like lightning crackling through a storm cloud. Lurking beneath the fizzing light show and sitting alone at a rogue desk in the middle of the hallway, was the balding man in the black turtleneck. He was once again massaging his brow in frustration. A soft moan hummed in his throat as he sat, hunch-shouldered and bent at the waist. His gaze lifted from the table and slowly, the terror that plagued his eyes leaked like mustard gas into the corridor. The sharp, familiar scratching sound hung about him as he once more dropped his head into his hands.

Becca choked on her breath, a jagged fishhook in her mouth, as she fumbled to form words.
"W…who… Who is he?" she barely managed to stutter.
Kayla shook her head and released Becca from her grip.
"We don't know," Kayla replied in a low tone, shooting Becca a stern look, "But he loves this show. We can't upset him. Ok?"
Becca had plenty of questions but realised she lacked the courage to voice any of them. Instead, she allowed herself to be pulled away from Turtleneck man's hawkish glare and found that she'd been led into the safety of an empty classroom. Marni slammed shut the door behind the three of them and let out a huge sigh of relief. She glanced up and caught Becca's eye.
"The genre of this show is *nineties teen drama*!" Marni admonished, "What the hell kind of teen drama do you watch where all the kids start beating the shit outta each other, huh? These kinds of shows are all about cheesy quips and showing up to the prom with the hot guy!"

Becca had slumped down at one of the desks and cupped her face in her hands.

"I don't really watch teen dramas; I like murder documentaries!" Becca admitted in a high-pitched whine, struggling to fight back tears.

She sniffed back the blockage in her nose in a grotesque snort and continued, "Who is that man and why am I here?"
Kayla pulled up a chair beside her and sat down.
"We don't know who he is, and no one knows how we got here,"
Becca's tongue seemed to swell in her mouth. She could barely breathe, and Kayla's horrifying admission hardly helped matters.
"No one ever remembers getting here. We don't know who or where we were before this place," Marni added, sure of herself that her words were helpful, "The lucky ones get to *stay* here,"
Kayla shot her friend a fiery glare and Becca's ears pricked up.
"What the hell does that mean?" Becca winced.

Kayla's eyes battled Marni's in a heated stare-down, until Marni eventually threw her arms in an exaggerated shrug.
"You may as well tell her!" Marni exclaimed, "She's here now, she'll find out eventually!"
Kayla's flame-filled eyes softened, and she massaged her temples with firm fingers. Becca's eyes grew wide.
"Look, kid. Sometimes…" Kayla sighed, roughly, "Sometimes people vanish."

Becca's jaw hung open.
"They vanish?" she asked, hoping that she had misheard.
Kayla nodded.
Marni added with a sardonic grin, "Yup. You always know it's going to happen too! People who are about to *go* start rambling about seeing *Them*…"
Becca glanced rapidly between the pair, her eyes wrinkled, baffled.

"*Them?*" she hissed, barely breathing.

Before she could get another word in, the harsh trill of the lunch bell sounded, signalling to the entire school that it was time to return to class. The classroom door burst open and around thirty people poured in. They were followed presently by a plump, bespectacled lady with greying hair that was slicked back into a neat military bun. Becca labelled her as the teacher, though given the broad age range of her new schoolmates; Becca saw no reason that this lady couldn't have been a pupil.

The greying lady took her place at the front of the room and cleared her throat loudly to address her class.
"Good afternoon children, I'm Mrs Carter!" she announced, "Today our topic will be…"
Her words were cut short by a surge of very familiar cheesy pop music.
"Oh, please God no!" Becca hissed in desperation. Her pleading went unanswered and the door burst open. A gentle cloud of fragrant smoke drifted into the classroom and with it, the music soared into a whimsical crescendo. Chad Wilding emerged from the mist like a superhero, his muscles rippling beneath his jacket and his strong jaw clenched in a deep smoulder.
"Oh God, I'm gonna headbutt a wall!" Becca hollered as she rose from her seat to escape the unbearable sickly quirkiness. Immediately, Kayla lunged forward, grabbed Becca's sleeve and dragged her back into her seat.
"Don't you dare draw any more attention to yourself!" Kayla snarled. Becca was slammed down into her seat once again and she buried her face in her hands. She couldn't bear to watch Chad snail his way to his desk for the next fifteen minutes. She was sure that if she had to listen to one more note of his upbeat *pop ballad* theme song, she would vomit in protest.
"Hey, pretty girl," Chad announced.

Reluctantly, Becca glanced up from her sulking to address him. Chad's perfect teeth gleamed as he smiled down at her, and his golden lion mane fluttered gently in a breeze that did not exist in any other part of the room.

"You didn't come to watch me play!" Chad said, unabashedly, "You should have come out, you would have had fun!"

The theme music that followed him had now softened in tone so that his voice could be heard over the melody. Becca curled her lip and retorted, "I'd have had more fun squeezing lemon in *me* own eyes!"

Chad laughed off her coarse remark, though Becca couldn't help but notice something troubling in his response. Hidden in his glorious peals of laughter was a small frown. It was a quick little thing but very apparent. It had clawed its way onto his lips, having cracked through the surface of his otherwise flawless exterior, a jagged fracture in the marble of his chiselled face. For the briefest of moments, pain sparkled in his starlit eyes, as though the world and its entirety of tribulations were weighing on his heart. As though the very soul within him was bleeding and wounded. The whole ordeal lasted less than a second before Chad's angelic demeanour repaired itself and he was once again smiling like a cherub. He shrugged as though nothing had happened and turned on a heel to walk away. His theme music surged in volume to symbolise this apparent momentous occasion, as he sauntered towards his desk in slow-mo.

Becca risked a glance around the classroom. No one else had noticed her unsettling exchange with Chad. She shrunk back into her chair and remained quiet; finally heeding Kayla's advice so as not to draw any further attention. She hunched her shoulders up to her neck and sat, unnerved, and shaken. After a few minutes of deep breathing, she felt somewhat calmer. She had just about steadied her shivering hands when, without warning, the sudden piercing screech of a record-scratch sliced through her ears.

Chad's theme music had ground to a halt.

The jarring sound had drawn the attention of the whole class and all were now steeped in a sudden crushing silence. Not a soul dared utter a word.

Chad stood silently. His head was hung low and he was staring at the ground. His whole body trembled, lightly at first, like a small leaf caught in an autumn breeze. It didn't take long for his hands to ball into quivering fists; clenched so tightly that it seemed his fingers would crack into shards. His whole body was now quaking so violently that he could have set the whole building atremble.

Mrs Carter attempted to inject some sanity into the situation. She stood from her desk and called out, softly, "Chad, why don't you take a seat, *huh*? You'd feel better if…"

"I can see them!" Chad hissed.

Mrs Carter raised her hand in a soothing gesture.

"Chad, dear? How about I get you a glass of water? And then you can have a nice *sit down*?"

Her voice was low and gentle, but beneath her soft tone was an unmistakable warble of panic. Chad's gaze snapped across the room like a bullet and his eyes, now filled with an unrivalled hellish fury, locked with Mrs Carter's.

"I CAN SEE THEM!" he bellowed, more a lion now than ever before, "THEY'RE COMING FOR ME! *MEEE..!* WHEN I'VE SUFFERED MORE THAN ANY MAN EVER HAS!"

"Chad!" Kayla was on her feet now, "*Chad*! You need to calm down! Just sit down and we'll work this out somehow! *Chad please…*"

"*SHUT UP, KAYLA*!" Chad screamed, cutting her off. He clenched his fists and took a rattling breath to steady his rage. He began once more, calmly, "How can they do this to me? When I've taken more bullshit than anyone else! I hate taking six hours to walk anywhere! I hate this crappy *feel-good* Top Gun music that follows me everywhere! Even my shits have a theme tune! NO MAN SHOULD HAVE TO TAKE A MUSICAL SHIT!"

Becca tugged desperately at Kayla's sleeve.

"Do something!" she pleaded but Chad was too far gone. He flipped his desk with the fury of a rampant ape, and he made a break for the door.

"*Chad, no!*" Kayla screamed but it was too late.

Chad never made it to the door.

His feet screeched along the ground as he skidded to a halt. His hand was outstretched, reaching for the door handle, though he remained frozen in place. He couldn't move. The violent quivering in his limbs was a clear indicator that this was not of his own doing. He wanted desperately to be free of his bonds. It was simply not in his willpower to do so. His body was a puppet in the hands of some invisible entity. He and everyone else knew it.

Slowly, Chad's arm returned to his side and he turned, deflated, to face his horrified classmates. With an audible *snap*, thick black fissures snaked up his once-perfect face, like cracks in a mirror. Suddenly, the fissures mutated grotesquely and soon they were thick and tangible tentacles. They slithered over Chad's entire body and abrasively enveloped him; a familiar scratching sound followed their every twitch.

Chad's skin drained from its healthy dewy glow to a sickly milky white. His limbs became stiff and ungainly, creaking violently under any attempt to move. The azure starlight of his eyes rolled away into complete blackness and sat in his head like perfectly polished suit buttons. He was calcifying. Chad's mouth dropped open weakly, as he willed his stony lips to form words.

"H...he...help!" he managed to finally splutter. But there was now nothing to be done for him. With one final sickening lurch, the black jagged tentacles clenched tightly around Chad's porcelain body.

The tremendous pressure was too much and finally, Chad violently exploded into stone pieces.

Chalk filled the room in a cloud of atomic ash, clogging and choking the screaming lungs of Chad's classmates.

All was chaos.

The class's howls of anguish ricocheted across the walls like gunfire as the dusty white shards of Chad's body dropped to an unassuming pile on the ground. The cacophony of screaming and wailing went unheard by Becca. She had retreated deep within herself; her mind had wandered elsewhere and only the dull thud of her heartbeat filled her ears.

"Oh my God," Becca felt her lips saying, "I can see them too!"

Kayla's head kicked to the side as though she had been slapped and her face drained of colour.

"Ignore it!" she ordered, her voice climbing with panic, "Whatever it is, ignore it! Don't leave us! Don't go!"

But Becca couldn't ignore it. Abstract shapes and vivid streaks of colour poured into the blind spot in her memory and suddenly, everything made sense. She blinked and her eyes were stabbed with a sudden, piercing white light. She blinked again. And again. Everything around her remained a startling white. When she halted her rapid blinking, she found that she was somewhere else entirely.

Becca was stood at the back of a large, white office. Her back was pressed against a wall and she stood trembling, cornered like a frightened animal. Far across from her, on the other side of the office, was a large wooden desk, piled high with stacks of paper and magazines. Perched at the desk, moaning softly in exhaustion, and massaging his brow, was the balding man in a black turtleneck sweater.

"I might have thought you'd show up," the Turtleneck man groaned without looking up. Becca's heart shrieked in her chest like a rusted bolt across an ancient door, and her mouth flapped uselessly.

"Of course, I've shown up!" barked another voice before Becca had a chance to answer. Becca's head snapped left, and she found herself, side by side, with a young woman in a crisp grey suit. Neither adult acknowledged Becca's presence. In fact, it rather seemed that they couldn't see her at all. Becca's mind raged into a sudden desert storm; her head stung from its coarse swirling columns of sand.

The young woman crossed to the desk, her high heels clacking with purpose and vigour across the hard floor. She slammed a hand down on the desk. Turtleneck man glared up at her in disgust.

He growled like a villain, "You can't just barge in here, you know? I don't accept anything you have to say on this matter!"

"The network hired me to boost ratings and here I am!" the woman spat back, "You have no choice but to take my changes on board!"

"Not like this!" screamed Turtleneck man as he reached beneath the desk. His hand returned, clutching a huge bound stack of papers, which he slammed against the wooden surface with a fury. The man flicked through the papers and stopped at a page near the centre. He brought down an accusing finger right in the middle of the crisp white leaf.

"You've cut Taylor from this season?" Turtleneck man barked, nearly frothing at the mouth, "Just crossed him right out? He was about to have a major character arc!"

The woman curled her lip, "Taylor the lab geek? You already had a plot thread with *Jimmy the lab geek*. It's repetitive and boring!"

"And what about this?" Turtleneck man seethed. He snatched up the manuscript from the table and held it out for the woman to behold. Becca craned her neck forward for a better look, though she didn't dare move from her space on the wall. She couldn't quite make out the words on that page, but she could see a harsh pen scribble. The black, jagged lines seemed disturbingly familiar.

Turtleneck man started in horror, "You've just completely... *completely*... erased Chad from the script! He's a fan favourite!"

"He is most certainly not a fan favourite!" the woman assured him, "Not these days. Audiences find him brutish and unrealistic!"

"And what about this damn British kid? She is completely ill fitting with this genre!"

"You mean Becca?" the woman spat with contempt.

Becca's lungs glowed with a sudden blue flame and smoke practically gushed from her nostrils.

"Me?" she whispered, hoarsely.

The woman in the grey suit remained undeterred, "This character is the subtle move into realism that this show needs. Becca was a character I had in mind for another show that got canned. She's too good to waste and is perfect to just slot into this show! It's a hill I'm willing to die on!"

Turtleneck man spluttered like a huge bald bird guarding a nest, "You very well may die on that hill, but I refuse to entertain this character in my show!"

Like a finely sharpened weapon, a large black marker pen was snatched from the desk, and Turtleneck man wielded it with a vengeance.

Becca's world glowed white once more. Her eyes focused only on that pen. There was nothing else in her sights. The pen did not move. It hung in the air, frozen in time. Even as it hovered there motionless, Becca heard a familiar, papery scratching sound. The sound of a pen furiously scribbling across a page.

Becca glanced down to her feet. Harsh black lines lassoed her ankles and snaked up her legs like the wanton vines of a carnivorous jungle plant.

"No…" her voice trailed off as the creeping black vines crept higher, biting at her legs with its inky barbs.

"NO!" she screamed, and her eyes clouded with grey smoke.

Everything faded to black.

****

Becca sat bolt upright at her desk. The cold air of the classroom was sharp in her chest as she glanced around in a whitewash of confusion and listlessness. She was still seated in Mrs Carter's English class with Kayla and Marni sat to either side of her. The once screaming and hysterical classmates, made frantic by the vision of their friend exploding before their eyes, were now subdued and bored by the monotonous droning of Mrs Carter's lecture.

Becca was dazed. She sat perfectly still, unable to move, apart from her rapidly blinking eyes. Eventually, she willed her arm forward and she popped open the lid of her desk. Becca reached inside for a small compact mirror. She hadn't known it would be there, just an educated guess. As she clicked open the mirror and gazed at her reflection, she saw that her face was no longer that of a sixteen-year-old girl's.

Instead, her gaudy blond braids had been freed into a wave of smooth honey locks, and her face now housed the defined, mature features of an adult woman. Becca glanced to the ceiling and steadied her breathing into a slow collected sigh. She turned back to Kayla.
Kayla was bewildered. Her knuckles were white as she clung to her desk with an iron grip. Her jaw hung agape as she regarded Becca's metamorphosis with horrified confusion. *"How...?"* she began, but Becca shook her head. Kayla needed answers.
'Where did you go?' she mouthed to Becca, *'What did you see?'*

Becca blinked her new eyes as she stared at her classmate. How could she put into words the things that she had just witnessed? How could Becca admit to her friend or even herself that the fabric of their entire universe was in fact paper? Their entire world was born of a pen in the hands of a balding screen writer. How could Becca say those words aloud to anyone?
The simple answer was that she couldn't.

Becca took a deep breath; laid her palms flat on her desk and with all the will that she could summon, she shot Kayla a bright smile. She beckoned to her and leant in close.

"Oh my god, did you totally see there's a new boy starting soon?" she asked in a stage whisper, her voice now a high-pitched, nasal American accent. Kayla's eyes sparkled with great bright tears, which she blinked away as best she could. She choked back her dismay and forced a toothy grin.

"Wow, that sounds cool!" she managed to say.

Becca nodded, slowly, her head clouding over as she fought with the single word that sat on her tongue.

"*Totally*," she said.

Easily Twisted

ACKNOWLEDGMENTS

Where to even start with these acknowledgments? Everyone in my life has been so overwhelmingly positive and have supported me on my journey to publishing.

This being my first project, I was certainly daunted. However, the encouragement that I have received has been amazing. The wonderful people below have all been equally invaluable and I will be forever thankful!

To my darling Owen, thank you for your continued support and encouragement. I will love you always.

To all the absolutely beautiful Gaskells and Gaskell-Swans, thank you for all your support and for reading the many drafts that I forced upon you!

Thank you to my mother Andrea, my bonus-father Graeme, my nana Christine, my grandad John, and my colossal baby brother Logan.

Thank you to my fabulous and many aunts, uncles and cousins – Uncle Matthew, Aunty Rachel, and cousins Alex and Ethan. Aunty Nicki, Uncle Karl, and cousins Claudia and Aemilia.

Simply put, I am surely the luckiest girl in the world to have a family as great as you guys!

Thank you to Supriya for giving me the idea to write a book of short stories in the first place! And thank you Todd for being a size 10 foot as always (leg…end…am I right!?) and making me laugh on the daily.

To my gorgeous girls, Ellis, Jade, Jenny and Kelly, thank you for your unwavering support, proof-reading skills, and most importantly, friendship.

Thank you to the two most gracious gentlemen of the clans McFaull and Isherwood, who never once failed to boost my confidence and make my day better. Thank you forever, Steen and Dan!

To Michaela and Fiac, thank you for being your wonderful selves as always, you have both filled my days with laughter and joy. I'm so glad you are both in my life!

Thank you to Ray and Sarah for being the brightest of stars in the darkest of times. Your support , as always, has been wonderful!

And of course, thank you to anyone that has been kind enough to pick up this book and give it a read. I hope you enjoy reading it as much as I did writing it.

Thank you.

REMEMBER, IT'S A TWISTED WORLD
OUT THERE...

BETTER STAY ON YOUR TOES...

More from this Author

Look out for

A Smile With Fangs

Coming soon…

Easily Twisted

3 Curiously Dark Tales to Keep You on Your Toes

JORJA GASKELL

Printed in Great Britain
by Amazon

86626767R00068